"I wanted you then, and I want you now…"

His kiss stole softly upon her unresisting lips, melting her will; his tongue brushed against her mouth, a flame that set the sensitive skin ablaze, challenging it to respond.

She scarcely knew that her arms had crept around his neck, or that her fingers were lost in the dark curls of his hair.

The moon poured its pure, pearly light into the silent courtyard. The faintest hint of a warm breeze was stirring the palm leaves, dappling the paving stones below with a criss-cross of trembling shadow.

And beside the rustling creeper, whose scented petals dropped from time to time on to the worn stones, was the perfect image of two lovers, clinging to each other, lost in a kiss that for one burning minute was touching eternity….

MADELEINE KER

the winged lion

Harlequin Books

TORONTO • NEW YORK • LONDON
AMSTERDAM • PARIS • SYDNEY • HAMBURG
STOCKHOLM • ATHENS • TOKYO • MILAN

Harlequin Presents first edition June 1984
ISBN 0-373-10699-8

Original hardcover edition published in 1984
by Mills & Boon Limited

CHAPTER ONE

ALEXANDRA Lacey tossed back her long, autumn-red hair.

'But I was going on leave next week,' she said resentfully.

Wilbert Carvel surveyed his young employee over the rim of his bifocals.

'It is a pity,' he agreed insincerely. 'But, after all, you can take your leave *after* the Castelnero job. And Venice will be so beautiful at this time of year.'

'Yes—but I was going to the South of France!'

'It's very overrated,' he assured her. 'All that blistering skin . . .'

'And I'll lose my deposit with the travel agent,' Alexandra added.

'Ah. Well, Carvel and Sons will pay any losses you incur,' said Wilbert Carvel, making a gallant effort to hide the pang that saying these words had given him. The forty-two-year-old Son in the firm of Carvel and Son, Fine Art Dealers and Restorers, was not noted for mad impulses of generosity.

Alexandra Lacey blinked her almost-violet eyes.

'You will? You must really want this job done!'

'Cataloguing and restoring,' Wilbert assured her smoothly. 'Nothing more than that. The simplest job in the world, my dear Alex—and think of all the culture you'll be absorbing!'

'Along with the damp,' Alexandra suggested wryly. 'What is Castelnero, anyway?'

'It's what the Italians call a *palazzo*. A big Renaissance apartment block, stuffed with dusty treasures and marble statuary.' He scooped up the thickish pink file that lay on his cluttered desk and

5

sorted through it eagerly. 'You see,' he went on, 'the place has been neglected for over a century. The last two members of the de Cassis family—they were the Princes who owned the place—were somewhat eccentric. Recluses, in fact—almost hermits. By the sound of it, the light of day hasn't penetrated the rooms at Castelnero since Gordon was killed at Khartoum.'

'You're not exactly filling me with enthusiasm,' Alexandra said with a wince. She could just imagine the cobwebby horrors and musty smells awaiting her. 'Look, Wilbert, I've been planning this holiday to the South of France for months——'

'Wait half a second before you say no,' Wilbert Carvel pleaded. There was a glint in his eye that made her heart sink. 'Now, Castelnero has passed into the hands of a gentleman called Anton de Cassis. He's the nephew of the last Prince, and rather more modern-minded. He's apparently spent most of his life in England.' Wilbert studied the crested notepaper in his hands. 'He went back to Venice to claim his inheritance, by the look of it.'

'This is all very romatic, Wilbert,' Alexandra sighed, 'but would you mind getting to the point? I've got three Victorian landscapes to clean. Before I go on holiday,' she added significantly.

'Of course, of course. Well, Mr de Cassis simply wants someone from this firm to go out to Venice and look through the collections there. He wants a proper catalogue made of everything there. He also wants any paintings cleaned that particularly need cleaning, and advice on any major restoration that needs to be done. You see?'

'But that could take months!' Alexandra's oval, undeniably beautiful face registered dismay. 'I'll never get to the Côte d'Azur! And I haven't had a holiday in three years——'

'It's just a routine job, Alex!'

She couldn't argue with that. Carvel and Sons specialised in cleaning and restoring precious artworks, often worth many thousands of pounds, usually extremely fragile, and almost always encrusted with dirt and age-darkened varnish.

It was an important and much-sought-after service —but not always an easy one to perform. A good restorer could double the value of an already priceless canvas. A bad one could ruin it for ever.

And when it came to the patient, knowledgeable restoration of oil paintings, Carvel's of the Strand had an enviable reputation. Alexandra had enjoyed her three years with the firm, and knew she had learned a great deal in that period.

But the prospect of missing her holiday in Antibes for the sake of another extended job, no matter now prestigious, was dismal.

'Why me, Wilbert?' she asked plaintively. 'Why not George? Or Suzie Watkins?'

'Because you're the best we've got,' Wilbert said with a cunning attempt at flattery. 'If we put Mr de Cassis off, there are a dozen other firms who'll snap him up.'

'I've had my holiday planned for months,' she said grimly, fixing him with reproachful, deep violet eyes. 'Turquoise seas and golden sands. That's what the brochure said.'

'But this is the opportunity of a lifetime,' said Wilbert, tapping the file. 'Mr de Cassis is quite prepared to let you stay at Castelnero for as long as it takes. He says so in his letter. And Castelnero is one of the finest Venetian palaces in existence.'

'I thought you said it had been shut up since the Dark Ages.'

'It'll be a marvellous experience for you. Besides which,' he added with a glint in his eye, 'that would save Carvel and Son your board. Which will offset the cost of paying your bill at the travel agent.'

'I'm so glad to hear that,' she said drily, 'considering that I don't even want to go there in the first place.'

'Isn't the prospect of six weeks in a magnificient Italian palace a lot more appealing than a few days on an overcrowded beach, getting sick on a lot of spicy foreign muck?'

'No,' said Alexandra. 'And I repeat—why me?'

'The answer,' grinned Wilbert, 'lies in your dim and distant past.'

'Oh yes?'

'Six months ago, you did a job for the National Gallery—minor cleaning work on four Canalettos.'

'So what?' she shrugged. But the first squiggle of excitement in her stomach told her that she was being very skilfully hooked.

'Antonio Canaletto was probably the greatest Venetian painter of the eighteenth century. You agree?'

'Of course,' she shrugged. Working on the four huge, wonderful paintings of Venice had been one of the most exciting experiences of her life. There was so much living detail, such wonderful light, such—' firmly, she stopped herself. 'So what?' she asked again, trying to look unimpressed.

'Well, I've been doing a little research,' said Wilbert smugly. 'When Mr de Cassis' letter arrived, I did a bit of poking around in dusty files in the British Museum. There are several large Canalettos which have never been accounted for, among them a view of St Mark's in Venice and a painting of Christ Church, in Oxford. Finding any of them would be a major event in the art world, Alex. Quite apart from the cultural value, a long-lost Canaletto would fetch a goodish price at auction. The last Canaletto sold at Sothebys,' he said, examining his fingernails negligently, 'fetched six hundred thousand pounds.'

There was a pause. Alexandra cleared her throat,

and casually adjusted her floral silk skirt over one slender knee. 'So what?' she repeated. But knew that Wilbert Carvel wasn't fooled by her show of indifference.

'So,' Wilbert smiled happily, 'the records show that the de Cassis family purchased a large painting of St Mark's during the early 1820s. The name of the artist isn't known. But an educated guess would lead us to——'

'Antonio Canaletto?'

'The painting could easily be hanging in Castelnero, dusty and forgotten, Alex. You're the only person in this firm who's actually dealt with Canalettos. You know his style, the sort of canvas he used, the kind of paint he preferred. You even know how the paint will have cracked over two hundred years——'

Wryly, Alexandra watched her French holiday receding on the horizon.

'—and if you *did* turn up a missing Canaletto, the reputation of Carvel's will be sky-high. As will your personal reputation. *And*——' he grinned, '—if Anton de Cassis asks us to handle the sale through a London auction house, our commission will be around fifty thousand pounds. Which means a very nice little bonus for you, Alex!'

'Yes. Always assuming that the Canaletto actually *is* there, mouldering under the cobwebs. Assuming that it hasn't been destroyed by rats and mildew if it does exist. And assuming that Mr de Cassis wants to part with it.'

'Quite. But you'll do it?'

'I need to think it over, Wilbert,' she sighed.

'Of course you do,' Wilbert said benevolently. His plump, rosy face was a mask of paternal affection. Which meant that he knew Alex was well and truly hooked. 'The last thing I want is to bully you into taking this job on.'

'I'm sure,' she muttered sardonically.

He passed her the file. 'It's all in there—my notes, Anton de Cassis' letter, the lot. Look through it, and make your mind up in your own time.'

'How long have I got?' she asked, hefting the file in delicate, long-fingered hands.

'Plenty of time,' Wilbert assured her, ushering her to the door of his office. 'I've booked you on the six-thirty flight to Rome tomorrow evening.'

'*What?*'

'First class, of course,' he said seriously. 'I want you to really enjoy this trip.'

'Talk about cheek!' Suzie Watkins exclaimed. 'All I can say is, I hope he treats our customers better than he treats his staff.' She looked at Alexandra, who was still poring over the Castelnero file. 'Are you going to go?'

'Does it look as though I have any choice?' She picked up the letter Anton de Cassis had written to Wilbert Carvel. 'Look at this.'

Suzie took the heavy, cream-woven paper and looked at the embossed crest at the top.

'Wow! Is this Anton de Cassis some kind of nobleman?'

'Your guess is as good as mine. I picture him as elderly, bald, and very pompous,' Alexandra shrugged.

Suzie was scanning the strong black handwriting.

'More businesslike than pompous, I'd say,' she judged. 'And what makes you think that he's not young, tall, and handsome?'

Alexandra arched one eyebrow over a sceptical violet eye. Gifted with her mother's stunning colouring, she had also inherited her father's fine, aristocratic bone-structure. The chestnut hair that bordered on auburn was long and heavily silky, and the eyes which were so deep a blue as to be almost mauve—'violet sapphires', a romantic boy-friend had

once called them—were made even more striking by a
fringe of glossy black lashes which never needed
mascara. The exquisite corner of her mouth tucked
itself into a wry quirk.

'Young and handsome? No such luck. I've given up
expecting miracles. What's more, the so-called palace
has been shut up since the Crusades. It'll be full of
rats and bats and spiders. But there *is* the chance of
turning up a Canaletto . . .'

'I'd love to go to Venice,' Suzie sighed wistfully.
Her open, round face was frankly envious. 'I never get
any of the glamorous jobs.'

'Poor thing,' Alexandra smiled. 'Why don't you take
my ticket to Antibes?'

'You don't mean that!' Suzie blinked.

'Why not? You've got some leave coming up,
haven't you? And I'd like to think that *someone* was
having a good time in the South of France while I was
poking about among the cobwebs in Venice.' She
grinned at Suzie's open-mouthed surprise. 'Go on. I
was only going to have to cancel it, anyway.' She
rummaged in her desk, and pulled out the colourful
airline ticket. She looked at it with a sigh, then passed
it over to Suzie. 'Bon voyage, Susannah.'

'Alex!' Impulsively, Suzie jumped up to kiss
Alexandra's velvety cheek. 'You really are a honey! I'll
pay it back to you somehow, I swear it——'

'Just have a good time,' Alexandra smiled, 'and toast
me in the champagne all those gorgeous Frenchmen
will be queueing up to buy you.'

'I don't have the luck you do, I'm afraid,' Suzie said
with a grimace. Though luck was scarcely the word,
she smiled wryly to herself, when you had been born
with a face and figure as lovely as Alexandra Lacey's.
There were always plenty of men ready to cast more
than a second glance at Alex's gentle, beautiful face
and slender figure.

The funny thing was that Alex herself seemed quite

unaware of her attraction for the opposite sex. She was modest, almost shy with men. And while her clothes were always perfectly chosen (or as perfectly chosen as Wilbert Carvel's not-very-high salaries permitted) they were never showy or overtly sexy.

One day, Suzie reflected, some man was going to awaken the light in those deep amethyst eyes, kindle the fire in Alexandra Lacey's heart. And claim all the love that was patiently sleeping inside her.

Just let him be a good man, Suzie sighed. There was a childlike innocence about Alex that just cried out to be taken advantage of. And the thought of generous, joyful Alex being hurt filled Suzie with horror.

'You are going to take care of yourself, aren't you?' she said suddenly, her plump face serious. Alexandra looked up in surprise, her eyes wide.

'I'm only going to Venice,' she smiled. 'You don't believe all those stories about Italian lovers, do you?'

'You bet I do! Anyway, just take care, okay? We don't want you being carried away by some Sicilian baron.'

'Don't we?' Alex looked wistful. 'I wish I could share your forebodings, Suzie. Or your enthusiasms, come to that. But I just know in my heart what this job's going to be like. Boring, damp, and musty. I'm going to take a hot-water bottle and a suitcase full of books to read.'

Although, she had to admit in the departure lounge at Heathrow the next evening, there was a certain thrill about being despatched to Venice at two days' notice.

Venice! The Pearl of the Adriatic. A city without streets or motor-cars, where beautiful women in furs rode in gondolas to the Doge's Ballroom.

And even though Castelnero was likely to be mildewy and mouse-ridden, it could hardly be very much worse than the tiny Pimlico flat she had occupied for the past three years.

In fact, as she peeped at her fellow-passengers over the edge of her *Vogue*, Alex had to admit that she was as excited as a child.

She had spent the last twenty-four hours reading every scrap she could find about Antonio Canaletto. And she had to admit that Wilbert's research had been spot-on. It was the kind of attention to detail that had made Carvel's of the Strand the leading firm in its field.

'Going on holiday?'

She glanced up at the middle-aged man next to her.

'No, business,' she answered, noting the sheen of anxiety on his balding brow. She had bought the copy of *Vogue* more as a defence against talkative male passengers than for the sake of something to read, and now she lifted the magazine up again, and pretended to be absorbed in the outlandish clothes the Japanese model was wearing on page 56.

'Me too,' said the balding man, undeterred. He tugged anxiously at his collar. 'You in the fashion business?'

'No,' she said uncommunicatively, then took pity on his evident desire to talk. 'Do you fly much?'

The other glanced out at the huge aircraft standing on the tarmac in the late afternoon sunlight outside.

'This is my first flight,' he gulped, then tried a shaky smile. 'I guess you travel by air all the time?'

'What makes you say that?'

'You just got the—the—well, the sort of glamorous look.' He looked Alex up and down, from the tip of her glossy leather boots to the swathes of autumnal hair she had tied so efficiently back. The roar of a Jumbo taking off outside made him wince, and Alex smiled.

'Thank you. But I don't fly a great deal, no.' Nor am I particularly glamorous, she had to admit. She had had to support herself since she was seventeen—the year in which Grandpa had died. After her parents' deaths while she was still a toddler, Grandpa had looked after Alex. With the help of Nanny, of course, an old Irish nurse with the face of a prizefighter and a heart of solid gold.

But Nanny had retired with arthritic joints, and a bare fortnight before her 'A' levels, Grandpa had suffered the first of two consecutive heart attacks that were to carry him off before the end of that year.

Wilbert Carvel had snapped Alexandra up at her first job interview. He had recognised in this shy, exquisitely pretty schoolgirl the sparkling intelligence and competence that his prestigious firm so badly needed.

Within a few short months, Alex was one of his best restorers, a young woman with an almost magical ability to bring a ruined piece of canvas and paint back to its original splendour. And now, three years later, Alex was the real mainstay of the small, prosperous London firm.

And Wilbert Carvel had nightmares about the day when Alex would come in to announce that she was leaving Carvel's to get married. Because there was no doubt that Alex was growing into a truly lovely young woman, a woman with a physical allure matched only by a delightful and witty personality.

And a gentleness that was now making a balding, slightly sweaty, middle-aged passenger-to-be feel thoroughly at ease.

'Sure,' he was saying, 'microlight aircraft are going to be a big thing in the future. GlasWings, my firm, are going to make the big time—yes, sir. I'm doing a route of six big European trade fairs over the next two months, selling our product. A hell of a lot of flying,' he remembered glumly, glancing at the round, Mickey Mouse nose of the Boeing outside. 'Oh, my lord!'

'Will all passengers board the aircraft now,' chirruped the air hostess, throwing open the sliding door that led along the boarding-tunnel to the aircraft's interior.

'Never mind,' Alex smiled as she and her companion joined the general movement towards the exit, 'it's not nearly as bad as you imagine. Personally, I love flying.'

'You do? I sure as hell wish you were sitting next to me,' sighed the balding man.

'It's all very routine,' she assured him, handing her ticket over to the stewardess. 'You'll probably be bored to death.'

But the exciting smell of travel that wafted from the interior of the aircraft had set her own nerves a-tingle. A smell of expensive perfume and aviation fuel, of smart clothes and leather and foreign places. A smell of vinyl and suitcases and freshly-printed magazines.

The late summer sun flooded the interior of the plane with golden light. Suddenly, Alex was very glad to be going to Venice. Very glad, and very, very excited. She sat down next to the Indian couple, and buckled the seat-belt over her light cotton suit, bracing herself for the thrilling roar and thrust of take-off. Ah well, she thought, so long, South of France. I guess Venice will have its own glamour.

It was a slightly less polished and more crumpled Alexandra who gaped out of the window of an Alitalia internal flight at the city spread out beneath them in the dying sunlight, two hours later.

Venice was surely the most incredibly beautiful city she had ever seen—from the air, at least. The setting sun made the criss-crossing of aquamarine canals glitter with silver and gold scales. A city that was actually a great island in the Adriatic, its streets canals, its walls the sea itself. A city of pale old-gold and rose-tinted granite, of domes and spires and castellated palaces, etched in the stunning Mediterranean sunlight that was somehow different from any other light on earth.

A city with a heart of water. A city intersected with blue water, set in a bed of blue water, outlined and rimmed and inlaid with sapphire water.

She could only gape, her eyes dazzled by the beauty of it all. After the comfortable dullness of two afternoon flights and several hours in a narrow seat, this almost Oriental sunset vision was bewilderingly lovely. She watched the basins and palaces pass beneath her in a kind of trance as the plane soared gracefully over the city to the airport at Mestre, the city on the mainland nearby. The sky was an unbelievably soft rose doré, edging into the blue-purple of an Adriatic evening, and as she followed the other passengers out into the balmy evening air, Alex was content to be in this delicious dream of beauty.

Wilbert Carvel had issued her with detailed instructions on how to get from Mestre to Venice, but she hardly bothered to consult them. The vision of Venice from the air had charmed her, utterly and totally, and she was more than willing to fall under its spell.

A spell that somehow glamorised even the elderly Customs official who examined the bottles and surgical instruments that were the tools of her trade with suspicious attention. A spell that brought a slight smile to her lovely mouth as she carried her bags towards the bus station.

The evening had settled in by the time she was sitting in the *vaporetto*, the water-bus, that was chugging towards her destination. But Venice was no less dazzlingly magnificent by night than by day!

Against the mauve and indigo of the evening, the façades of Venice stretched like strings of precious jewels. The pearls and diamonds of their lights were reflected in the dark water, and the floodlit façades had the enchanting quality of a very high-class opera set.

Except that this was fact, not fantasy.

'*Ti piace Venezia?*' smiled the pilot, noting the awestruck expression on the English girl's face.

'*Si,*' she breathed, staring at the majestic towers and Moorish basilicas. 'Yes, I think I'm going to like Venice very much.'

The party of American tourists who had travelled with her since Rome were all at the windows of the *vaporetto*, exclaiming at the beauty of it all. Alex shared their joy without wanting to look any closer. There would be time enough to study the stones of Venice one by one; for now, she was drinking in the first impression of this utterly magical place. The motor-launch glided under a floodlit bridge, a poem in marble and granite that she remembered having seen in a thousand photographs. She did not know its name, but one of the Americans supplied it for her.

'That's the Rialto,' the pigtailed girl called eagerly. 'Isn't it terr*ifi*c?'

'It's marvellous,' Alexandra smiled. 'I've never seen anything like it.'

'Me neither. Say,' the American exclaimed, clambering over on to Alex's side of the seat with childlike pleasure, 'that must be one of the great ballrooms!'

She turned to follow the pointing finger, and through a long row of stately first-floor windows, caught a glimpse of row upon row of dazzling chandeliers, lit up like frozen fountains. Above the putt-putt of the *vaporetto* they caught the strains of a graceful waltz; and now Alex noticed that the waterfront at the steps of the huge *palazzo* was thronged with boats and gondolas, a glittering assemblage of expensive pleasure-craft.

'Tonight is the Midsummer Ball,' a Venetian passenger informed them with the pitying patronage Venetians reserve for anyone unfortunate enough to have been born abroad. 'All the great ones of Venice are here tonight, dancing, playing, making love . . .'

'What do you know,' Alex's companion breathed in

wonder. 'It's Midsummer Night in Venice! My God, look at those chandeliers—and those boats!'

They stared silently at the magnificent scene drifting by. The huge foyer of the building was as bright as day, and thronged with people. As though in a fairy dream, they caught a glimpse of satin and taffeta and velvet. Alex fancied she could even see the diamonds that dripped from the cool white throats of the women and smell the cologne on the men's tanned cheeks.

And then the scene was past them, and the *vaporetto* was chugging up the Grand Canal towards the Rio Foscari. The American girl sighed like a contented child.

'Wasn't that something?'

'It certainly was,' Alex agreed gently.

'Is this your first time in Venice?'

'Yes. Yours too?'

'Yep.' The little blonde stuck out a friendly hand. 'My name's Kitty Kowalski. Pleased to meet you.'

'Alexandra Lacey—Alex for short. Pleased to meet you, Kitty.' She met the merry blue eyes of the other girl, liking her instinctively.

'I hope we'll see you around,' Kitty was bubbling happily. 'It's going to be fabulous, isn't it? I'm touring with my college friends.' She jerked a thumb at the other girls, who were clustered in the stern, trying to photograph the vista down the canal. 'We're staying in the YWCA. Where are you staying?'

'As a matter of fact——' Alex began, but the *vaporetto* was pulling into a 'bus station' at the side of the canal.

'*Signorina!*' The pilot waved to Alex, then pointed up at the building opposite. '*Ecco* Castelnero—your stop.'

'Well,' smiled Alex, groping for the handles of her bags, 'this is where I'm staying, apparently.'

'You're kidding!' Kitty Kowalski's pretty little mouth dropped open as her round blue eyes surveyed the majestic façade that towered over them. 'You're staying *here*?'

'So it seems,' Alex nodded, struggling with the bulky cases up the narrow aisle. 'I'll try and drop round at the YWCA some time. Otherwise call here and ask for me.'

'You're kidding,' Kitty Kowalski said again, her expression leaving Alex in no doubt that she had made a significant impression!

She clambered on to the steps, taking the bags as the pilot passed them to her, then turned to stare up at Castelnero.

And had to agree with Kitty's amazement. Castelnero, from the outside at least, was very far from the decaying mansion she had expected. The venerable exterior was in splendid condition, and four cleverly-placed floodlights illuminated its grandeur beautifully.

The whole first and second floors consisted of two long loggias, guarded by rows of marble pillars separated by pointed Moorish arches. Above, a series of Renaissance statues was poised above the intricate marble-work; and the remaining two floors of the palace were covered with patterned brick and ceramic tiles. It was a fantastic and impressive place, made all the more mysteriously beautiful by the soft light that glowed behind the intricate windows. This was no crumbling ruin, but a living treasure.

'Say!' Kitty Kowalski was calling from the departing *vaporetto*, 'Alex Lacey! Meet you at the "Y" tomorrow lunchtime. Okay?'

'Okay,' Alex shouted, and answered the cheery wave. The glowing façade of Castelnero loomed above her.

How on earth had it acquired such a gloomy name? *Castelnero* meant 'black castle', and this place was a symphony in honey-gold and white marble.

Shaking her head in slightly numbed admiration, she picked up her bags and trudged up the huge staircase to the studded wooden door, set in a forest of stone leaves.

She pressed the bell, her heart beating heavily against her ribs. It was beginning to occur to her that Signor Anton de Cassis might be as different from her mental image of him as his palace was!

Supposing he was young and handsome, after all? What a tale that would be to tease Suzie Watkins with! The deep internal chime of the bell was answered by footsteps, and then the great oak door swung open.

To her intense disappointment, the man who stood in the great doorway was well past middle age, white-haired, and despite the fine black suit he wore, very far from attractive.

The brown eyes that surveyed her inquisitively, however, were friendly enough.

'Signor de Cassis?' she ventured timidly.

'You must be the young lady from Carvel and Son,' the man said, his voice pleasantly accented. 'Come in, come in.' He took her bags, and led her into the almost overpoweringly wide and high hallway.

Alex found her gaze irresistibly drawn up past the marble figures in their niches to the softly-glowing chandelier above, and the vaulted, magnificently-painted ceiling beyond.

Any ideas she might have had that Castelnero was a mildewed and decaying ruin evaporated in that instant, to be replaced with wonderment and awe. This place was truly a palace, a palace that embodied all the magnificence of Venice past and present.

She dropped her wide-eyed gaze to the elderly man opposite her.

'I'm so sorry, Signor de Cassis,' she smiled awkwardly. 'I'm just overcome by all this. I never expected——'

'It is wonderful, is it not?' The other agreed. 'But I'm afraid I am not Signor de Cassis. I'm Signor de

Cassis's private secretary.' He bowed with old-world dignity. 'My name is Umberto Borghese.'

'Alexandra Lacey,' she rejoined, not certain whether or not to offer her hand. Umberto Borghese nodded.

'Welcome to Castelnero, Signorina Lacey. I'm sorry to say that Signor de Cassis is out tonight. He asked me to make you as comfortable as possible, and to convey his greetings to you.'

'Thank you,' she said somewhat formally, still a trifle daunted by the Baroque magnificence of the place.

'You must be tired and hungry after your journey,' the elderly secretary said. 'The cook has made some salads for you. Would you like them in the dining-room? Or shall I have the maid send up a selection on a tray to your bedroom?'

'The dining-room sounds a little grand,' said Alex with a tentative smile. 'A tray in my room would be fine.'

'Certainly,' Umberto bowed. 'Now—may I take you up to your apartment?'

Apartment? Dumb, she followed the slightly stooped figure across the huge hall. A touch on a button, and the intricately-carved panels of a doorway opened to reveal the plush interior of a small lift, gleaming with mirrors.

'For some reason,' Alexandra volunteered wryly, 'I was under the impression that this place was in a state of neglect.' She watched the steel doors slide silently closed. 'I had no idea that Castelnero was as magnificent as this.'

'The palace was indeed badly run down,' Umberto informed her. 'When Signor de Cassis acquired it last year, it was on the verge of disintegration. Signor de Cassis has had the whole building restored and modernised. This lift is one of his improvements.'

'He certainly gets things done,' Alex smiled. She

glanced covertly at the old man. 'What does Signor de Cassis do, if I may ask?'

'He has several business interests,' the secretary smiled. 'The Principe Emmanuele Gandolfo, who died some eighteen months ago, was his uncle. Signor de Cassis returned from London to inherit Castelnero on the Principe's death.'

'I see.' The lift doors opened smoothly on to a wide corridor, beautifully panelled and hung with oil paintings. As she followed Umberto Borghese to the wide double doors at the end, her curiosity got the better of her.

'Signor de Cassis,' she probed, 'is he—er—an elderly gentleman?'

'Elderly?' The secretary smiled, shaking his head. 'Oh, no. Signor de Cassis is thirty-six. I have known him all his life.' He threw open the doors. 'Your apartment, Signorina Lacey.'

Alexandra stopped with a little gasp. The apartment was nothing short of palatial. It was unmistakably a woman's suite, decorated and fitted out to suit a woman's delicate taste. The thick carpet was a pearly grey, matching the grey and cream panelling and the heavy, lustrous rose-grey drapes at the windows. Four small chandeliers illuminated the main chamber, which was deliciously spacious. The furniture was fine, white, and slender-legged—apart from the satiny sheen of rosewood here and there—and the *salone* was equipped with escritoires, delicate Japanese cabinets, and a wonderful Rococo divan, exquisitely carved for some sultry beauty to recline on as she held court.

Various cream-inlaid doors led, doubtless, to a bedroom, a bathroom, and what Alex guessed would be dressing-rooms or cupboards.

Umberto Borghese glanced at her silent face with concern.

'You don't approve?' he asked. 'Signor de Cassis

thought you would like the Ivory Suite. But if you would prefer something more cheerful——'

'Oh *no*,' she breathed, finding her voice at last. 'This is exquisite, Signor Borghese.' She stepped into the room almost timidly. 'Simply exquisite!'

'Excellent!' beamed the old man happily. He hefted the bags over to one of the doors as Alexandra stared around her in delight.

By heaven, Wilbert Carvel had been right! To think she had almost turned all this down for three greasy weeks in Antibes!

'I'll send one of the maids up to unpack your suitcases,' Umberto promised. 'Would you care for some wine with your dinner?'

'I'm intoxicated enough with the splendours of Venice,' she smiled, and the old man's eyes lit up.

'You have fallen under its spell already? Excellent! Some mineral water, then?'

'That'll be perfect.'

'Very good, *signorina*. Now, if there's anything you require——' he pointed to an ivory telephone, it's ultra-modern fascia harmonising strangely with the Venetian Renaissance desk on which it lay, '—simply pick the receiver up, and someone will answer.' He glanced around to make sure that nothing was out of place. 'I'll leave you for the present, then. Goodnight, Signorina Lacey—and once again, welcome to Venice!'

CHAPTER TWO

As the door closed gently behind Umberto Borghese, Alex gazed around her with bemused eyes—and noticed for the first time the huge vase of yellow roses on the little mahogany desk. The fragrance of the flowers was delicious, and their vivid, youthful colour seemed to illuminate the pale, exquisite tints of the *salone*.

Beyond one of the doors, as she had guessed, was a bedroom. The four-poster, canopied in pearl-grey silk and covered with a cloud-light feather quilt that could scarcely be needed on these warm summer nights, was one of the most splendid pieces of furniture she had ever seen. But not the most chaste. The little cupids carved into the fine wood left the viewer in no doubt that this was a bed made for other things than sleep!

And on the wall beside it, a large oil painting of a voluptuous nude reinforced the atmosphere of witty, elegant eroticism. In the other part of the room, a serpentine dressing-table and stools flanked the doorway to a bathroom.

A bathroom with a solid onyx bath let into the floor. A bathroom tiled in Florentine ceramic, with gilt taps shaped like dolphins. A bathroom aromatically scented by the fragrant leaves of the pelargonium which grew abundantly against the window, its white-and-green sprays drooping prettily over the bath and creeping gently around the marble nude of a faun which knelt gracefully behind the taps.

'Oh, goodness!' she whispered. Her fascinated reverie was interrupted by the entry of a black-and-white uniformed maid who was setting down a silvery tray in the *salone*.

'*Buona sera, signorina,*' the young girl curtseyed, her brown eyes lifting shyly to survey Alex's deep blue eyes and auburn colouring, so unusual in Italy. 'Shall I unpack your bags now?'

'Yes, please,' Alex nodded. After all, when in Venice—She picked hungrily at the delicious salads as the maid put her clothes away with efficient skill. 'What's your name?'

'Bettina, *signorina.*'

'Please call me Alexandra, Bettina.'

'Very well, Signorina Alexandra,' the maid smiled shyly. 'Shall I put these dresses in the cupboard?'

'Yes, please.' Wryly, Alexandra reflected that the clothes she had brought were not exactly going to match her opulent surroundings. Still, no doubt the mysterious Anton de Cassis would expect her to work in jeans and old T-shirts, rather than a mink coat!

'Bettina,' she ventured, 'do you happen to know where Signor de Cassis has gone to-night?'

'Of course, Signorina Alexandra,' smiled the other woman. 'He has gone to the Midsummer Ball at the Doge's Palace.'

'Of course,' Alex said drily, toying with a celery stalk. With all the other great ones of Venice. Dancing, playing and making love . . . 'With whom?'

'With the Princess Marina Bergatrice,' supplied Bettina. She paused with an armful of lingerie, her little heart-shaped face alight. 'Oh, she is so beautiful, that one! She and Signor de Cassis make such a wonderful couple. They will get married soon, I am certain!'

'Really?' Alex crunched the crisp stuff thoughtfully.

'Oh, yes, Signorina Alexandra. Signora de Cassis is really a Prince, you know. He refuses to use the title—but he has a right to it.'

'Indeed?' Alexandra watched the little maid's busy back. 'Is he handsome?'

'Like a god,' said Bettina with a little sigh, and

shut the cupboard door gently. 'Will that be all, *signorina*?'

'Yes, thanks—you've been very kind.'

'It was nothing,' smiled the girl. 'Goodnight, *signorina*. Pleasant dreams!'

'*Grazie.*' Like a god? Well, that was unequivocal enough! Alex shook her lustrous hair out of the decorous bun she had tied it into, and brushed it into the thick, heavy curls it always insisted on forming.

Her tiredness had slipped off her like a travel-stained cloak. She felt refreshed, happy. And it was only ten-thirty.

By now, the Midsummer Ball would be at its dazzling height, the couples whirling round the huge dance-floor like bouquets of flowers in a whirlpool . . .

Suddenly she wanted to explore Castelnero a little more. There was always the excuse that she was making a professional survey! In reality, she was consumed by curiosity. The house was empty, and the master at a ball. Now might be her only chance to really wander through the palace, looking where she chose, dreaming where she chose . . .

She slipped out of her suit and boots, and into a pair of cotton pants and a cool, sleeveless blouse. Pulling on a pair of canvas sandals, she wandered happily out of her stately apartment and down the silent, magnificent corridors to the lift.

The paintings were, as she now could see, for the most part extremely dirty. But not seriously so—her skilled eye told her that most of the grime would come off with a gentle rubbing of pure turpentine. One or two of the older paintings were so dark as to be almost impenetrable, though. She decided to avoid the lift, and walked down the ten-foot-wide staircase into the hall below.

Wouldn't it be wonderful to find that Canaletto? she thought with amusement. Just hanging there, above the jet-trimmed clock. Or above that heavily-arched doorway.

Across the empty hall, she found herself in the dining-room. It was a long, rather imposing chamber, dominated by one vast oil painting which looked to Alex suspiciously like a Rubens. Could it be?

'My God,' she whispered, 'this place must be worth hundreds of thousands! Maybe millions . . .'

She passed on to the drawing-room beyond. Here, the atmosphere was more intimate. Behind the heavy curtains, the windows looked out through the loggia on to the canal, now thronged with gondolas and *vaporetti*. The satinwood furniture had been upholstered in a fine rose damask, a colour which was echoed in the pink tints among the buttermilk-coloured panels and the gorgeous colours in a large oil painting of a sunset which hung over the wide fireplace.

As she turned on the chandelier, rose-tinted drops among the crystals picked up the colour scheme, and brought the room to beautiful, warm life.

Alex wandered among the wonderful furniture reaching out to trail her fingers against the cool sides of a Chinese vase or the intricately-cut gold of a table-clock, feeling like a child let loose in a museum.

She had wandered, just like this, in stately homes and palaces in England. Behind ropes, of course, and under the watchful eyes of guards. Picking up information about her craft. And she had always wondered what it must be like to actually *live* in such a setting.

Well, now she was going to find out. She smiled at her mental picture of Castelnero as a decaying, rat-infested old wreck. This place was——

A rustle in the doorway made her spin round in surprise. And with an almost physical shock, found herself staring into the smoky, stunningly beautiful eyes of the most handsome man she had ever seen.

The eyes were grey, the cloudy blue-grey of a panther's, and their large, dark pupils were fixed on her with a mixture of surprise and amusement. The long lashes which made their impact even more shockingly direct were jet-black. Like the level brows and the thick, crisp hair that framed a bronzed, magnificently male face, whose authoritative, sensual mouth was now curving into a quiet smile.

'Good evening,' he purred, walking into the room, his hands in the pockets of a dinner-jacket that had been cut with aristocratic elegance. 'This is a very pleasant surprise. Miss Lacey, I presume?'

'That's right,' Alex said numbly, unable to drag her eyes away from his. 'I—I'm afraid you've caught me snooping——'

'Not at all. My house isn't a museum. And you are an honoured guest.'

'Am I?' faltered Alex. He was tall, and under the impeccable suit, his body was obviously fit, hard, and powerfully made. He stood with the slender-waisted grace of a matador, but there was a mature strength to his shoulders and thighs that made him an almost intimidating figure. 'Are you Anton de Cassis?' she asked hesitantly.

'At your service,' he agreed urbanely. His smoky eyes dropped to make an unabashed male appraisal of her figure—an appraisal that was somehow infinitely flattering, and not in the least insulting. Which didn't prevent the faint flush from spreading into Alexandra's cheeks as she dropped her eyes. The man had a magnetic presence, an atmosphere she had only experienced in one or two of the charismatic, famous people for whom she had done restoration work. It was almost the dangerous challenge one felt in the presence of some big hunting cat.

'I thought you were at the Midsummer Ball with the Princess Marina Bergatrice?' she said, trying to cover her confusion.

'The Princess Marina was foolish enough to eat a dish of prawns,' he smiled gently. 'And she has an unfortunate allergy to shellfish. I have just this minute returned from escorting her home with a face like a giant strawberry.'

The gentle irony of his deep, caressing voice made her giggle despite herself. Anton de Cassis was utterly male, utterly beautiful—and utterly sophisticated. There was little trace of sympathy in those purring tones.

'And I, for my part, thought you had retired to bed,' he said. He walked with leopard-like grace over to a silver tray of bottles that stood on a sideboard. 'I'm very glad that you decided to stay up.' The smile that he threw her sent a quiver of excitement along her veins; there had been an unmistakable wicked undertone in that apparently innocent statement. 'Please sit down, Miss Lacey. And what can I offer you to drink?'

'Oh. Er—a Campari with soda, please.'

'That sounds nice,' he approved, making the drinks. 'I'll join you.' She sat down rather weakly, watching his deft movements at the sideboard.

There was a challenging grace about the way he moved; or perhaps it was something in his nature that set the whole room alive with electricity. Whatever it was, Anton de Cassis was someone very special.

And it wasn't her numbed brain that told her so. It was something else, some inner, female instinct that probably went back to the days of caves—a sixth sense that told her, as surely as any logical thought, that this was a real man, a man with an inward power and purpose.

He turned from the sideboard, the two ruby-filled glasses in one hand, and once again those magnificient eyes jolted her.

'Your Campari.' He raised his own glass slightly,

smiling down at her with an intimacy that made her pulses flicker. 'To you, Alexandra Lacey.'

'Thank you.'

She sipped the bitter liqueur, relishing its fragrant impact on her palate. Anton de Cassis sat down in an armchair opposite her, and stretched out long, elegant legs.

'I had no idea that the efficient Mr Carvel was going to send such a beautiful woman to Castelnero,' he smiled, his eyes warm on her.

'Does beauty conflict with efficiency?' asked Alex, slightly rattled by the compliment.

'Not at all,' he grinned. 'In fact, the two ought to be synonymous.'

His teeth were white, even, and beautiful. Instinctively, she knew that no dentist had rearranged them; like everything else about this man, they were simply perfect. Does he have any idea, she wondered numbly, how stunning his smile his? And what effect it's going to have on every woman within a hundred yards?

'I'm sorry your evening at the Ball was interrupted so early,' she ventured rather formally.

He shrugged, undoing his black bowtie.

'These things happen. A pity—I wanted to dance tonight.' He unfastened the top two buttons of his silk shirt, revealing the golden-tanned column of his throat and the first crisp black curls at the top of a muscular chest.

Suddenly, he was not a sophisticated *bon viveur*, but a sheer male animal, vibrant with erotic allure. The exquisite cut of his jacket and white waistcoat only emphasised the animal sexuality of his presence.

Fleetingly, Alex wondered whether some woman's hand somewhere had chosen the superb clothes—and then knew that the answer was no. No sane woman who had a stake in this superb male creature would dream of choosing clothes that showed off his powerful and elegant sexuality so effectively!

'In any case,' he continued, 'there will be other dances. Welcome to Venice, Miss Lacey, and welcome to my house.'

'Thank you.'

'You've been studying the paintings?'

'Just superficially,' she said, embarrassed. 'To tell the truth, I wanted to look around the house on my own. I hadn't the slightest idea it was such a wonderful place—your secretary told me that you had to do a lot of restoration?'

'Yes. Castelnero had been shut up for a long time, and there was much that needed doing.' He drank, his eyes watching her over the rim of his glass. 'It was once one of the most famous of the Venetian *palazzi*. Do you find it a trifle museum-like?'

The question caught her off guard.

'Not—not really,' she stammered.

'No? You looked like a child lost in a museum, Miss Lacey.' She looked away from his smile. Damn him! How had he known that that was exactly how she had felt?

'It's a beautiful place,' she said woodenly. 'I'm looking forward to working here.'

'Good.' He smiled again, and this time the charm was impossible to ignore. She couldn't stop herself from smiling in return as she met those amused, bright eyes. 'You must learn not to be shy, Miss Lacey,' he said gently.

'Shy?' she quavered. She had thought to have left that behind years ago! Nature had cursed her with a shyness and reserve that she had always had to struggle with. But three years at Carvel's had taught her how to cover her awkwardness with a layer of poise. Or so she had thought. 'I thought I *had* learned not to be shy,' she grimaced. 'Does it show?'

'Only because you're so beautiful,' he informed her calmly. 'In a plain woman it wouldn't matter—no one would study you closely enough to notice.'

'I don't think that's a very nice thing to say——' she began huffily, then broke off as she realised she was being gently teased. 'Oh. A joke?'

'I'm sorry,' he said gravely, 'I was pulling one of your elegant legs. Of course, every woman has her own fascination, her own allure. And that will prove irresistible to one man in the universe. One man, at least—no matter what she looks like.' He drank. 'But to return to your shyness—I must contradict you, Miss Lacey. I don't think you've ever learned not to be shy. You've learned how to disguise your shyness—which is quite a different thing.'

'I see,' she replied formally, inwardly cursing his alarming perceptiveness. 'And pray tell me, Signor de Cassis, how does one learn not to be shy?'

'*Nosce te ipsum*,' he said silkily. 'Know thyself. You are very beautiful, Alexandra Lacey. Beautiful, and I have no doubt, capable. Why should you be shy, then?'

There was pink in her cheeks as she met his eyes. 'Because I can't help it,' she snapped. 'And I was brought up to believe that a person's external appearance hasn't got anyting to do with their real worth as a human being.'

'You've been well brought up, then,' he smiled. 'I wasn't referring to your external appearance, though. When I said you were beautiful, I meant something more than your adorable mouth, your sparkling blue eyes——' he toasted her with his glass, '—and your magnificent hair.'

Feeling distinctly hot, Alex clasped both hands round her own glass to steady them.

'What can you possibly know about my character, Signor de Cassis?' she queried sceptically. 'You've only just met me.'

'Time is relative. Haven't you heard of Einstein? Time isn't all the same, Miss Lacey, like the sands of the desert. Time has oceans and currents. It has whirlpools and tides, it has great chasms, and it has infinite wastes.'

'Do you really believe that?' she asked, shuddering.

'It's true,' he said gently. 'And at some very special, very rare places in life, time stands still. In those places, my dear Alexandra, logic does not follow its usual course. A man and a woman can learn everything there is to know about one another in the space of a heartbeat. The impossible happens as a matter of course.'

'And you——' She paused, spellbound by his words. 'And you think that this—this is one of those places?' she asked breathlessly.

'Don't you feel it?' he smiled. 'Here in this room, on Midsummer Night, time has come to a stop for us. There's no one else in the whole world. No Venice outside those windows, no teeming millions, no galaxies beyond. Just you and I, and our beating hearts.'

She put her hand to her throat, almost shaken by his mysterious teasing, her deep blue eyes wide.

'I could go to the window,' she whispered. 'And if I looked out, I'd see the gondolas and the lights——'

'Of course.' His eyes were fathomless, the smile in them tender and elusive. 'As soon as you want it to, time will begin to move again. But wouldn't you rather remain awhile in this silent lagoon with me?'

'You frighten me when you talk like that,' she said in near-alarm.

'Don't you feel the truth of what I'm saying?' he challenged quietly. 'Don't you feel that this is a special meeting, a special place in the web of the universe?'

'I don't know,' Alex said restlessly. She locked her fingers together, and met his eyes beseechingly, as though this man really were in control of the ebb of time! 'If you don't mind,' she pleaded, 'can we talk about something else?'

'Nothing else is remotely as important,' he said with

a slow smile. 'But—as you wish. Go to the window—you'll see that the earth is still spinning round.'

The cheerful hoot of a barge came distantly from the river outside, breaking the spell. Alex sighed, as though some charm had been lifted.

'You mustn't tease me like that,' she said with a touch of dryness coming back to her voice. 'I'm just an ordinary woman, Signor de Cassis.'

'Ordinary?' he queried, lifting one eyebrow. 'I think not, lady of the red-gold hair.' He considered her, his cloudy grey eyes thoughtful. 'You are not like other women, Miss Lacey.'

'No?' She forced a smile. 'What am I like, then?'

'Shy,' he smiled. 'We've decided that. But not a shyness that comes from being gauche or uneducated. Rather, a shyness that grew out of loneliness. You also have that special calm, that tranquillity that only the lonely can know. Yet you are too beautiful to have been ignored by men. So I guess that no man has moved you yet. And no woman, either, perhaps.' He searched her now-pale face carefully. 'You have few friends. You live for your work—your career, in which you intend to go far. Emotions frighten you, even the pleasant ones. And yet, inwardly, you hunger for love like a woman dying of thirst. You dream, in your most secret moments, of what your logical mind assures you will never be—the true love that is every woman's right. And because you insist on listening to your logical mind, your confidence ebbs away. You tell yourself that you aren't interested in men, that they're not interested in you. And that keeps you lonely, calm, high above the noise of the common world.' He drained his glass, and looked full into her eyes. 'How am I doing?'

She couldn't answer. Her fingers were shaking as though she'd witnessed some witchcraft. How could he know so much about her? How could he possibly have searched her heart in such detail, with such piercing accuracy?

'Not bad,' she said—but now it was her throat, not her voice, that was dry. She touched her lips with her tongue to moisten them. 'How—what made you say all those things?'

'I learned them from your heart,' he said calmly. 'Did you think I was playing with you when I said that this was a special meeting?'

'I——' Her voice petered out. She gulped, trying to reassemble her scattered wits. She mustn't let this man get the upper hand, for heaven's sake! 'I think I'd better go to bed,' she said, touching her temple with icy fingers. 'I'm very tired now——'

'You see?' he purred. 'You feel it too. Time stood still for you—and now you're paying the price.'

'I didn't know there was a price,' Alex said in a low voice.

'There's always a price,' he smiled. 'But sometimes it is ecstasy to have to pay it. Have you seen the Hall of Mirrors yet?'

'I don't think so——'

'Come on, then, before you go to bed. I want you to see it now.'

Uncertainly, she stood up and took the arm he offered her. Under the fine material, she was acutely aware of living, hard muscle. Being next to him was a strangely intoxicating experience; as he led her to the doorway, she was aware of his animal grace next to her. She could feel the warmth of his body, an electrical presence that made the fingers she rested so lightly on his arm tremble slightly. Dimly, she listened to what he was saying.

'John Ruskin stayed at Castelnero for six months. That was in its heyday, of course. Later, he wrote of the Hall of Mirrors here, "Versailles itself has nothing more magnificent to show." I wonder how you're going to react.'

There was a slight smile on his lips as he opened the high doors to the next room, and reached out to the bank of switches against the wall.

As the great Murano crystal chandeliers burst into blazing life high in the vaulted and stuccoed ceiling, Alex felt her senses sway, and her fingers dug into the arm of the man beside her.

The vast room was a bewildering, dazzling cavern of gold and crystal. As her eyes recovered from the initial shock, she slowly began to take it in. The walls, which were completely covered with golden and ivory arabesques, were set with immense, soaring mirrors, each one framed in intricate gold and decorated with garlands and the sweep of golden silk curtains. The sense of space which the endless reflections provided turned an already majestic, wonderful room into something unbelievable, as unreal as a princess's dream.

'Come.' Gently, Anton de Cassis led her into the hall. The floor was covered in blue and yellow marble tiles, set in beautiful geometric mosaics, and all around the sides of this huge chamber, carved giltwood furniture in the Rococo style stood silent and majestic.

Anton de Cassis glanced at her wide, dazzled eyes, then tilted her chin up with a gentle forefinger.

'Look at the chandeliers. They're Murano glass—over ten thousand pieces of crystal in each one.'

'Heavens!'

She stared upwards, transfixed, into the heart of the silent, frozen explosion of diamonds above her. The bewildering skill of the maker had somehow created the impression of a cavern of ice. The thousands of multi-faceted teardrops quivered slightly, each shedding splinters of turquoise, ruby and topaz light into the overall fountain of luminous beauty . . .

The tall man next to her watched her face, his grey eyes dwelling on her satiny skin, on the soft, full lips that were now parted in wonder to reveal the soft pearl of even teeth.

Alex scarcely noticed as his arm slid around her shoulders, drawing her towards him, so that his mouth could descend gently upon her own.

She closed her eyes in the first shuddering ecstasy of his kiss. His lips were warm, demanding. Their strength moulded her softness, taking a deliberate, sensual pleasure in savouring the sweetness of her delicate skin.

Imperceptibly, his arms drew her closer as their kiss deepened in intensity. With spinning, delicious giddiness, she felt his mouth brush against the soft inner skin of her lips, pressing gently and firmly against her teeth, pressing them open.

The real world was melting around her, dissolving into a multi-coloured dream of gold and rainbows. And as though her very bones were melting, too, Alex felt her body swaying against him, her feminine curves moulding themselves to the hard, sculpted power of him.

It was the first time any man had ever kissed her like this, the first time that her logical mind had been outwitted, deposed by the magic drug of her senses. She had suffered, never enjoyed, the clumsy kisses of the boys who had taken her out. But that had been different. Those damp, puppylike caresses had been revolting, at best laughable.

This intoxication was the mature desire of a mature man. Something she had never dealt with before, and something that she was unable to cope with. She scarcely knew that her own slender arms were entwined around his neck, or that her fingers were running luxuriously through the thick, crisp curls of his dark hair.

She felt that every muscle in her body had been suddenly electrified—and then drenched in some exquisite narcotic that seemed to dissolve her body into honey, warm honey that ached to be tasted, savoured, devoured.

Her long lashes parted slightly, languidly to see his tanned cheek, her own fingers stirring in his hair. She could feel his hands sliding sensuously down her slender flanks, drawing her even closer to him.

And above, the dazzling, frozen explosion of light in the vast chandeliers.

The piercing sweetness of his kiss was like a golden sword that sank deep into her, a pleasure-pain like nothing she had ever known or imagined. The power of this man, his virile authority, were overwhelming. His maleness was a force which made her weak, dizzy; a force that was almost frightening in its intensity, urging her to surrender utterly to this superior will, this infinitely greater strength.

And then consciousness returned, slowly and agonisingly. With a supreme effort, she slid her hands on to his chest, and pushed him weakly away.

Her intoxication gave way to a growing anger, directed both at her own weakness and at his presumption.

'Is this how you always seduce your women?' she asked in a low, trembling voice as she withdrew from his embrace.

His grey eyes were dazzling.

'I'm sorry,' he said softly. 'I should not have done that.' He allowed her to step away from him, a slow smile playing on the passionate lips that had been kissing her so recently. 'You've no idea how beautiful you looked, Miss Lacey, gazing up at the chandeliers. Your eyes are a wonderful, deep blue—almost the colour of forget-me-nots. And your lips were shining, and parted so invitingly——' he reached out a forefinger to brush her full lower lip, his eyes smiling into hers, 'I'm afraid I simply couldn't resist such a delicious prospect.'

For an instant she swayed towards him, his potent

spell overwhelming her again; and then reason struggled to reassert itself. She turned away, trying to hide her breathlessness.

'Well,' she said bitterly. 'I've had a taste of Venetian gallantry, at least.'

'Half Venetian,' he purred. 'My mother was an Englishwoman. Don't be so angry, Miss Lacey—there's really no need for it.'

'I'm not angry,' she replied with a pretence at calm. Their image was reflected in a hundred glowing mirrors, again and again—the tall man in evening dress, one brown hand on his hip; the slender woman with the long, autumn-red hair, turned slightly away from him to hide the turbulence she knew would be showing in her deep cobalt eyes. 'I simply like to choose who kisses me, and when.' She drew a deep breath, pulling her blouse straight with shaking hands, and mustered the courage to turn and look at him.

His level grey eyes held a glint of deep amusement, though the magnificent face was calm.

'I shall try to remember that,' he said smoothly.

A spark of anger stung her into a quick retort.

'Are you laughing at me?'

'No,' he said gravely. 'Not very much, anyway.' He smiled, two bewitching quirks appearing at the corners of his mouth. 'To speak quite frankly, Miss Lacey, at the moment I'm desiring you quite intensely.'

Alex gulped, knowing that he was fully aware of the shudder his words had set off inside her.

'I think I'm going to bed now, Signor de Cassis,' she said unevenly. 'I'm very tired——'

'Not yet,' he said quietly. And there was a command in his voice that stopped her more effectively than any order. 'It is, after all, Midsummer Night, Miss Lacey. Every woman ought to dance at least once on Midsummer Night.'

'But——'

'We even have a ballroom,' he said, gesturing at the

Baroque splendour of the Hall of Mirrors around them. 'All we lack is a little music.' With lithe steps, he walked over to a massive giltwood cabinet against one wall and threw its doors open. Inside was a nineteenth-century victrola, its elegant horn beautifully engraved in chased gold. He wound it up, grinning at her. 'This belonged to poor Nicholas,' he told her.

'Nicholas?' she asked, bewildered.

'Nicholas II, Tsar of all the Russias. The Bolsheviks killed him and his family in 1918. This was his personal gramophone.' Reverently he placed a record on the beautiful old turntable. 'I'm afraid it isn't high-fidelity stereo,' he murmured, almost to himself, 'but somehow I prefer its tone in this room.'

He walked towards her, one hand outstretched. The hiss of the ancient record-player suddenly gave way to the surprisingly lovely strains of a Tchaikovsky waltz. The bittersweet, heart-tuggingly nostalgic sound rose up to the vaulted ceiling, filling the whole vast ballroom with its evanescent beauty.

'But——'

'Come.'

Before she could resist, he had swept her into his arms, his smile as dazzling as the great chandeliers over their heads. Her mind numb, Alex found that her body was moving with his to the time of the waltz.

He danced superbly, with a sheer grace that astounded her. He had the mastery, the control of a great dancer, so that they were instantly dancing as one person, the power and suppleness of his body guiding her own feminine delicacy.

It was like magic exploding in her veins, this wonderful movement, this oneness. It was impossible that she had known this man for barely an hour; in her heart she felt that she had known him for ever, had danced with him a hundred times, a thousand times before.

And in answer to that strange feeling, the glittering mirrors on the walls showed her a thousand images of herself in his arms as they whirled by.

His hand against her back pressed her taut body close to him as they danced, alone beneath those blazing chandeliers. She was aware of his tense stomach muscles against hers, the brush of his hard thighs against her own; and beneath the hand she had placed on his shoulder, she could feel the living pulse of his muscles, like liquid steel against her slender fingers.

'Your eyes are really hyacinth,' he said softly, his gaze intoxicatingly deep upon her. 'And your hair—it's the colour of the woods in November, the colour of autumn fire. I don't think I've ever seen such a beautiful face, Alexandra Lacey. I had imagined you as an elderly spinster, I must confess.'

'And I imagined *you* elderly, balding and pompous,' she had to smile.

'You dance beautifully,' he said softly.

She threw her head back, so that her long, gold-tinted hair streamed out behind her, and laughed gently.

'It's you, not me, who is the superb dancer. I'm just following you, *signore*!'

And indeed, it was though her feet scarcely touched the floor. She was whirled along in his power like an autumn leaf on a rushing river, her mind lost in the giddy delight of the music.

Bittersweet music, music that told of the end of a great Empire, of a lost, glorious period before the world knew violence and upheaval. Music to which Nicholas and Alexandra might have danced, under other chandeliers than these, under the opalescent spectrum of the Northern Lights.

'Are you really going to marry the Princess Marina?' she asked, the words coming out before she could stop them.

'Now who told you that?' Anton de Cassis enquired, coming to rest in the centre of the floor as the music faded into silence.

'The maid—Bettina.'

'One thing you will have to learn in Venice,' he said as he turned to walk back to the victrola, 'is never to listen to the gossip of servants.'

He paused to look back at her across the great hall, a supremely male, supremely elegant figure utterly at home in this Baroque setting.

'Shall we dance again?'

'Yes,' she whispered.

This time, the music was Franz Léhar, pungent and full of gypsy excitement—but carrying the same nostalgic atmosphere as before.

Alex drifted in his arms, light as thistledown, dimly aware of his body close to hers. The exhaustion of the day and all its events was beginning to catch up with her. She was beginning to feel like Cinderella—that if she didn't get to bed soon, all this magic would abruptly cease, and leave her alone and shivering.

A delicious langour had spread through her body. The dancing and the sweet music had soothed all the tension from her limbs, and her voice was slurred slightly as she looked up at him.

'I'm so very sleepy, *signore* . . .'

'You'll be able to sleep all you want,' he smiled. 'It is, I'm afraid, the shortest night of the year. But I'll make sure no one disturbs you tomorrow morning.'

She hardly heard him. Her arms were twined unashamedly around his neck, and her lovely head drooped against his chest, her cheek warm against the silk of his jacket, her glossy hair brushing his chin.

Cocooned in the warmth of their closeness, she leaned against him, her body against his. The record had long since finished, and only the prolonged hiss of the needle remained, like the sound of the distant sea.

Anton de Cassis held her in his arms for a long

minute, looking down with thoughtful eyes at the thick lashes resting against the satin of her cheek. Then he kissed her very gently on the forehead, and sliding an arm about her waist, walked with her to turn off the record-player and extinguish the blaze of the chandeliers.

Alex was barely awake as the great Hall of Mirrors slipped into darkness, and her weak legs stumbled on the Persian carpet.

With a soft laugh, he scooped her legs up and carried her in his arms to the marble stairs.

Weakly, she tried to protest, but he ignored her. With no more effort than if she had been a child, he carried her up the massive stairs to her bedroom.

'I'm so sorry,' she whispered. 'I'm just so very tired . . .'

'There's no need to apologise. At least you danced on Midsummer Night.'

The bed he laid her on was deliciously soft and welcoming. He unfastened her sandals, then laid the quilt over her, fitting the pillows under her head.

'Goodnight, Alexandra,' he said quietly. His lips were warm on her own, his kiss as light as a feather.

'Thank you——'

'I'm very glad you've come to Castelnero,' he said, and she could hear the smile in his voice. Laboriously, she tried to open her eyes.

Then she heard the door close quietly, and sleep swamped her thoughts with a dream of crystal and gold and white marble.

CHAPTER THREE

A LANGUID Alex blinked her way into wakefulness the next morning among the tumbled glory of her hair.

The sun was streaming through the high windows and filling the ivory-tinted bedroom with morning gold as she sat up, blinking away the delicious, elusive dreams that had enveloped her. She was still in her blouse and cotton pants, now creased into un-respectability, and when she checked the watch on her wrist, it was barely nine.

Fifteen minutes later, Alex was revelling in the scented bubbles of a morning bath. The onyx tub was wonderfully smooth on bottom and back, and the marble faun peeped at her mischievously through the aromatic leaves of the pelargonium.

She soaped herself with the yellow disc of precious heliotrope soap she had found, rinsing away the sleepiness and dreams and languor of the night. Her body was beautiful, her skin satiny and the colour of honeyed cream, except where it deepened into the roseate tips of her rather full, upward-tilted breasts. She was slender-waisted and long-legged, and the rich cascade of auburn hair swayed past her shoulders as she clambered out of the bath, setting off the glow of her skin beautifully.

The wide, rose-tinted mirror confronted her with her own image as she towelled herself dry, reminding her of that extraordinary meeting with Anton last night. What if he could see her now, bare-breasted and shameless, her long legs planted gracefully apart as she towelled her back? The thought made her grin quickly, and there was a slight flush on her cheeks as she turned away from her own voluptuous reflection to dress.

By some psychic intuition, Bettina was setting breakfast out in the *salone* as she pulled on her dress. It wasn't exactly what she would have chosen to wear to start work on a gallery of dusty paintings. The deep blue voile was patterned with Paul Klee-esque designs in turquoise and robin's egg. The sleeves were airy and cool, and the almost wispy material had a tendency to cling to her figure as she moved. It also set her eyes and hair off dramatically.

And in her heart she knew that she wasn't dressing for work. She was dressing for Anton de Cassis.

And the tune she was humming as she brushed her lips with the merest suggestion of pink gloss was a Tchaikovsky waltz that had been playing in her dreams all night.

'Your breakfast is ready, Signorina Alexandra,' Bettina called, and Alex allowed herself to be lured out by the scent of fresh coffee and hot croissants.

But she was in a more sober mood as she brushed the last crumbs off her lips. Last night had been a dazzling, wonderfully romantic experience. But at all costs, she had to stop herself from being dazzled by it.

Anton de Cassis was someone outside her sphere, out of her reach. With a face and body like that, he would have conquered hundreds of women in his thirty-six years. Women more beautiful, more accomplished, more worldly than she.

The thought made her wince.

It also drove home the message that her mind was giving her heart. Don't get involved. Don't fall in love.

Okay?

Just do your job, stay out of this magnificent prince's way, and get back safely to Carvel and Son, Fine Art Restorers, and your tiny, safe Pimlico flat. Venetian princes and solo waltzes at midnight on

Midsummer Night are for Venetian princesses. Not twenty-year-old London girls aching for first love.

If some angel had looked into her innermost heart, and been commissioned to create the most exciting, most perfect male lover for Alex Lacey, the ensuing creation could scarcely have matched Anton de Cassis. For he was not merely mind-bendingly attractive—that in itself might have been bearable—but he was also brilliant, charming, cultured. All the things that she had looked for in past boy-friends, and had never found.

They had all been boys, mere children, compared to this man's intelligence. Anton understood her in a way no other man had ever done. He seemed to know the thoughts in her heart, seemed to understand her desires, her secret dreams. He probably even knew exactly how powerfully the sway of his magnetism pulled her.

And she knew exactly what her grandfather would have said about him. He's not for you, child. He has the pick of the most eligible women in Europe to choose from. Walk away, Alex.

While you still can.

She sat, thinking about it for a few minutes, knowing that it wasn't going to be easy to avoid Anton de Cassis' spell. And knowing that, unless she was going to be prepared for heartbreak and destruction, she must avoid it, must run from it, hide, anything.

Bettina peeped round the door.

'La signorina e sérvita?'

'That was a lovely breakfast, thank you,' Alex smiled.

'The master instructs me to say that he will be away this morning,' Bettina recited as she gathered the porcelain. Confidentially, she added, 'He has flown down to Milan for a big conference with some French businessmen. They want to buy his new designs. Umberto told me.'

'His designs?'

'For a television satellite.' Bettina glanced at Alex. 'Didn't you know? Signor de Cassis is one of Europe's most brilliant designers of telecommunications equipment.'

'I didn't know that,' said Alex, her azure eyes thoughtful. 'I guess he's very rich?'

'Oh, *signorina*! Have you heard of Telescan?'

'Of course.' She had seen the logo and the name dozens of times at the end of television programmes and in the headlines of the financial section of the newspapers.

'That is his company, *signorina*. Only one of his companies. He is very brilliant.'

Bettina's little sigh left Alex in no doubt what her personal feelings were about Anton de Cassis. She smiled at the Italian girl.

'Is he a good man to work for?'

'He is an angel,' said Bettina emphatically. 'When my sister was ill in Napoli——'

But the arrival of Umberto Borghese interrupted Bettina's tale, and she skipped off with the tray as the elderly secretary came in to greet Alex.

'I'm ready for work, Umberto,' she said gaily, and he smiled.

'Signor de Cassis has had a special studio set up for you, Signorina Lacey. And of course, you are absolutely free to work on whatever takes your attention. Shall I show you to it?'

'With pleasure. I'll just get my bag of tricks.'

And a few minutes later, Umberto was showing her into the airy top-floor studio where she was to work. A number of sensible oak desks were arranged in the spacious, sunlit room, and a stack of dusty canvases was propped against one wall, ready for cleaning.

The old thrill of her trade gripped her at once, and as the secretary left her, she was already setting out the bottles of cleaner and swabs she was going

to use, and eyeing the paintings with the light of
battle in her eye.

As a first measure, she checked through the
canvases, setting aside the ones that looked as though
they were going to be easy to clean. None of them
looked remotely like a Canaletto. Several of them,
however, were distinctly intriguing, and pinning an
apron over her dress, she set to work at once. As she
had anticipated, the majority of the canvases were
in good condition, and she was able to remove most
of the accumulated grime with a careful application
of mineral turpentine. It was rewarding work. Whoever had collected these paintings had shown excellent
taste. She must remember to mention the possibility
of the existence of a Canaletto to Anton de Cassis. It
wasn't unlikely that there were other paintings stored
in cellars or box-rooms.

Within an hour and a half, she had four beautiful
little landscapes arranged on one of the benches. One,
at least, looked as though it might be a Claude.

They glowed in the light, drying off. The paint
had the characteristically tender look that recent
restoration brings, and she knew she had done an
excellent job on them. If the rest of the works in
Castelnero were going to be as simple as these four,
her stay here was going to be shorter than
anticipated. She rang for coffee, and considered her
next patient over the fragrant cup.

But the fifth painting she tried was a different
proposition. It was one of the largest of the canvases,
set in a beautiful hand-carved frame. It was the frame
which attracted her attention in the first place, since
the canvas itself was almost impenetrably dark. She
could barely distinguish some kind of figure-study
beneath the sticky brown residue of ages. But that
frame suggested that this work was much older than
the others, and possibly more valuable.

And that little glow of excitement in her heart as she

lifted it gently out of its frame was what made her love her work. The thrill that told her she might—just might—be on to something interesting.

'Everything all right?'

She looked up at Umberto, who had brought up a tray of marzipan biscuits to go with her coffee, and smiled.

'Fine. What do you think of my handiwork?'

'Signorina Lacey,' the old man exclaimed, coming forward to examine the four landscapes, 'you are a magician! You've transformed them!'

'Just restored them,' she admitted modestly, laying the fifth canvas down on the newspaper-covered bench she was working on.

'This whole house is going to be transformed by your arrival,' the old man chuckled, bustling out of the door. Alex set to work again.

Choosing an inconspicuous corner, she rubbed at the surface gently. Turpentine made no impression. It was evidently time for Alexandra's Potion—as her own special mixture was known at Carvel's. It was a mixture of turps and various wood alcohols that she had evolved herself. The fluid had strong dissolving properties, and in inexpert hands could be fatal to a fragile painting. But Alexandra Lacey's long-fingered hands weren't inexpert.

Slowly, the brown stain lifted under her swab. A beautifully-painted golden tassel—perhaps the corner of a cushion—was revealed beneath her fingers.

Cheered, she propped the painting up so she could get at it more easily, and set to work cleaning the whole surface.

It wasn't particularly quick work. Within half an hour, the top third of the painting had been cleaned.

And the laughing face of a beautiful brunette was looking back at Alex from the canvas. Her dark eyes glittered with a knowing, almost voluptuous amusement.

'Hullo there,' Alex whispered to the unknown model. 'Welcome back into the light of day.'

Her cleaning had revealed the woman's naked body as far as the tops of her creamy breasts. The background, a dark velvet couch strewn with lilies and roses, was becoming clear.

Delighted, she studied the area she had cleaned. Late seventeenth century, by the look of it, and maybe a truly major artist's work.

'Bronzino?' she wondered to herself. 'Maybe even Caravaggio? Let's see the rest of you, my fine lady!'

The artist, whoever he was, had obviously enjoyed an intimate relationship with this model. Only affectionate knowledge could have enabled him to capture her saucy grace so delightfully.

'I wonder who you are?' she murmured softly, rubbing at the surface with skilled fingers.

'By the look of her,' said a purring voice behind her, 'one of my less reputable ancestors.'

Her heart was suddenly racing as she turned to meet Anton de Cassis' bright grey eyes. He was wearing a beautiful dark grey suit with a slim red tie and a white carnation in his buttonhole.

And there was a spray of butter-yellow roses in his hand.

'For you,' he smiled, laying them on her lap, and leaning over her to inspect the half-cleaned nude.

'Thank you,' she said breathlessly, charmed by the gesture. She could smell the musky tang of his aftershave—Gucci?—and by daylight his magnificent face was even more stunning.

'Do you recognise her?' she asked, not sure whether his closeness was alarming or exciting.

'Ginestra de Cassis,' he said. 'I think so, anyway. There are other portraits of her downstairs—we'll have a look later.' He tugged at his lower lip, staring at the canvas. 'You are very talented, Alexandra. I didn't believe such a transformation was possible.'

His use of her first name hadn't escaped her, and to hide the flush it brought to her throat, she turned back to her work.

'She's very beautiful, at any rate,' she said. 'Was she a princess?'

'Mmmm. 1640 to about 1700.'

Under her fingers, the model's breasts had now appeared, tipped with delicate pink nipples. Which didn't help the blush that had now settled hotly in her cheeks. Why, oh, why hadn't he come in while she was doing a harmless landscape?

'Was your trip to Milan a success?' she asked, trying to sound relaxed.

'Yes. The French can be surprisingly businesslike, though. In my experience they're a lot more canny than the Scots.' He perched himself on the desk beside her, folding his arms, and watched her with opal-bright eyes.

'Umberto told me you've lived in London?' she probed.

'I was born there. My father was very Anglicised; he never had very much to do with his brothers. They, in any case, had inherited the family titles. My mother was an actress—so I had a very English, very democratic upbringing.'

'Really?' There was nothing democratic about him now, she thought wryly. She had never seen a man who so stunningly combined an aristocratic presence with physical comeliness. 'I wasn't aware that you owned Telescan,' she said, her violet eyes fixed firmly on her work.

'Ah. Telescan rode to success on the S.T.R. The so-called Scientific and Technological Revolution,' he explained with a smile. 'Micro-circuits, etcetera. It was just my good fortune to be in the driving seat.'

'More than fortune, surely,' said Alex, meeting his eyes briefly, and then bending assiduously over

Ginestra de Cassis' slender waist. 'You must have known what you were doing.'

'I suppose so,' he agreed indifferently. And she realised intuitively that this man had a purpose and direction that was nothing to do with looks or physique. It was an inner force that would have made him pre-eminent in whatever field he had decided to choose.

'And you?' he asked. 'May I ask how old you are?'

'Twenty?'

'Twenty? And already so lovely? By thirty you will be like the Sphinx,' he teased gently, 'slaying men with those hyacinth eyes! What led you into art-restoring?'

'I'm a failed painter,' she confessed. 'I love art, but I realised at a very early age that I didn't have the talent to fulfil myself. So I prefer to make other people's work more beautiful.'

'You showed a lot of self-knowledge for a young girl,' he murmured. Alex looked up.

'I had a childhood that predisposed me towards self-knowledge,' she said simply. 'My parents were killed in a car-crash when I was still a child, and my grandfather brought me up in a little house near Theydon Bois.'

'Were you lonely?'

'Sometimes.'

'I lost my parents when I was in my teens,' he told her. 'First my father, then my mother.'

'I'm sorry. And after that?'

'A few years drifting. A degree. Some struggling. And then Telescan.' He shrugged his broad shoulders.

The model's delicate navel had appeared by now, and there seemed to be a little cat or dog curled against her, in the curve of her hip. Anton's sharp eyes had caught it.

'What's that?' he asked, pointing to the dim blur. 'Can you bring it out?'

Alex obeyed. A sleek black cat appeared, its lazy emerald eyes staring out of the painting at them.

They both laughed at the delightful touch, then met each other's eyes. There was something in his gaze that made her stomach muscles contract, sending a jolt of high-powered electricity surging through her.

Anton de Cassis was certainly the most marvellously handsome man she had ever set eyes on—more handsome even than that Renaissance portrait she had fallen in love with in her late teens.

It was the eyes, deep grey and set off by dark lashes, which hit you first; but his mouth was no less fascinating. It was, she now knew, a mouth to quell and conquer, a mouth full of character and authority. But the sensuous lines in which it was etched promised shuddering pleasures for the quelled and conquered!

A straight nose, firm, high cheekbones and a virile jawline completed a face that might have belonged to Mars. Like a god, Bettina had said.

'Signor de Cassis——' she began quietly.

'Anton,' he corrected, his eyes fathoming hers, seeming to touch something deep inside her and melt it.

'Anton,' she said, his name like cognac on her tongue, 'I'm afraid I can't work with you sitting there.'

'Do I disturb you?' he asked softly, his voice a caress that lifted the fine hairs on her arms.

'Yes,' she confessed, trying to control her voice, 'you do.'

'Good. Because you disturb me, Alexandra Lacey. You disturb me very much.' He reached out to brush her shining auburn hair, a touch that made her eyelids flutter closed.

Alex took a deep breath, laying down her swab of alcohol.

'I think I'm going to break off for lunch now,' she said unevenly. His eyes were locked on hers.

'Have lunch with me,' he offered. 'At the Lido.'

'I'm afraid I can't,' she replied, standing up and avoiding his eye. 'I promised to meet an American girl at the YWCA—we met on the *vaporetto* from Mestre.'

And she didn't know whether she was bitterly disappointed at having to refuse him, or relieved at having an excuse to escape his disconcerting presence.

All her good resolutions about being wary of Anton de Cassis had suddenly evaporated, like morning mist in the heat of the sun.

'I see,' he smiled, coming close to help her take off her apron. For a dizzying moment his arms were around her supple waist, and she felt his body against hers.

Nor did it help her that she sensed his disappointment under that calm manner.

'Perhaps you'll meet me for an *aperitivo*, then? Take the afternoon off. You've done wonders enough for one day. And I'll meet you—and your American friend, of course—for a drink at the Lido. Shall we say five-thirty?'

'That sounds lovely,' she said sincerely.

'Good.' He turned to cast one glance at the three-quarters-finished portrait of Ginestra de Cassis. 'You're very good,' he said softly, his brows coming down over grey eyes. 'Very good indeed. I hope we can find enough work to keep you here at Castelnero, Alexandra. For a long time.'

She watched him walk out, her mind spinning with his smile.

'The thing is, I know next to nothing about him. All I know is that every time he looks at me, or comes near me, or smiles—well, my heart just starts doing somersaults.' Alex threw a handful of corn at the glossy pigeons crowding around their feet. 'I've never known anyone like him. And I just don't know what to do about it.'

Kitty Kowalski, who had been staring across the huge square at the immense Cathedral of St Mark as she listened, turned shrewd blue eyes on Alex.

'You like him?'

'Well, isn't that obvious?' Alex retorted. 'I think he's magnificent!'

'Sure.' Kitty sprinkled the last of her packet of corn among the scuffling, plump pigeons. She took Alex's arm in an unexpectedly firm little hand, and led her through the throngs of tourists towards the clock tower that dominated the other side of the square. 'C'mon, Alex. I want to show you something.'

It was a beautifully hot summer afternoon, the sky an intense blue above them, and the famous square was crowded with happy sightseers, Venetian and foreign alike. Alex and Kitty had lunched at a *trattoria*, and had found their initial liking for each other rapidly turning into friendship.

'Look up there.'

Alex followed Kitty's pointing finger up at the massive campanile. Beneath the great bronze bell, set in front of a majolica frieze of golden stars against a blue background, stood a huge statue of a winged lion. One massive paw rested on an open Bible, and his sweeping wings curved open above his broad back. Beneath him, passive under his power, lay a globe of the world.

'Know what that is?' Kitty asked. 'That's the winged lion of St Mark. The winged lion of Venice.' She glanced at Alex's face. 'This town may be just a beautiful tourist attraction now, Alex, but once Venice was a major power in the world. "Once did she hold the gorgeous East in fee", and all that. Venice was a great maritime empire. And to this very day, there's a custom that they enact every year, on Ascension Day. The Doge and all the nobles and notables sail out into the Lido seaway in a golden barge. The Doge throws a wedding ring into the sea, and says, "We wed thee, sea, in token of our perpetual rule." '

'That's fascinating,' said Alex, her brow slightly creased in puzzlement. 'But——'

'You said this Anton de Cassis was magnificent, right? Well, that winged lion is magnificent, too. Isn't he? This whole Venetian Empire business is magnificent. Magnificent and powerful. And dangerous.'

Alex stared up at the huge creature above them. A little smile tugged at the corners of her mouth, though her eyes were serious.

'Are you trying to give me a subtle warning off, Kitty?'

'You're dern tootin', kid! Look, Alex, I don't know where you stand in English society. I mean, maybe you're really Lady Somebody with a thousand acres in Gloucestershire, or something. But to me, you seem like a very nice, *ordinary* girl. This Prince de Cassis comes from a line of rulers who thought nothing of executing a few thousand rebels here or there or seizing any odd little princedoms that were going spare from here to Asia Minor.'

'Anton——'

'May be an angel in human form, sure.' Kitty grinned, patting her companion's arm. 'Take a tip from a girl who's seen the rough side of love—and just make sure those wings he carries you off on are angel's wings. And not lion's wings!'

'And how do you tell the difference?' Alex smiled as they strolled back towards the aquamarine-blue waterfront.

'That's up to you. For all I know, your friend may be as nice as pie. But—well, can I be horribly blunt?'

'Go ahead.'

'Don't go jumping into bed with him, until you're sure in your heart that you know what you're doing.'

'Kitty!' Alex laughed in mock-horror. 'What makes you think I go jumping into bed with *anybody*?'

'You reckon you can resist Signor de Cassis' charms?'

'Of course,' Alex grinned. 'I'm not exactly a child any more.'

'No,' Kitty said drily, glancing at Alex's beautiful face. 'But I can tell the signs, chum. You've got stars in your eyes, and I know who's put them there.'

They had reached the colourful striped posts at the waterfront, where a fleet of sleek black gondolas bobbed on the tide. A clamour of competing gondoliers rose up as they paused, choosing their craft.

'Just watch yourself, Alex, that's all. And as for Signor de Cassis—well, I'll give you my expert opinion once I've met him.'

'I look forward to that,' Alexandra smiled. 'Now, let's forget winged lions for a bit, and just see Venice. Okay?'

'That's what we came for. Which gondolier do you prefer?'

'The one with the red ribbon in his hat.'

'An excellent choice, mademoiselle. Shall we trip?'

They stepped into the boat, arm-in-arm, happy.

But despite Kitty's solemn warnings, Alex could tell that she was as utterly stunned by Anton de Cassis as she herself had been, when, some two or three hours later, they found themselves at a sunlit table overlooking the Lido. Anton's grey eyes were watching Kitty gravely as the American girl extolled the virtues of Venice.

'It's the most *mar*vellous place,' she was saying, fluttering her eyelashes at him over her Dubonnet. 'I think you're so *lucky* to live here, Signor de Cassis!'

'I only live here for part of the year,' Anton corrected her. 'I have a house in London and another near St Tropez. I like to spend part of the year at each. And please call me Anton.'

'Anton—what a *love*ly name! And I do think St Tropez is fabulous——'

Wryly, Alexandra sipped her Buck's Fizz and watched Kitty Kowalski falling under Anton's spell.

Did all women, she wondered, become so transparent in his presence? She was going to tease Kitty mercilessly about this shameless flirtation later on.

'Now,' Anton purred, stirring the ice in his Campari, 'tell me what you've seen today.'

'Well——' began Alex, but Kitty rushed in.

'We saw St Mark's—that was just stunning—and then we took a gondola to the Rialto—my God, what *prices* they charge!—and then we——'

Anton's eyes met Alexandra's with a glint of amusement, and then he turned seriously to the little blonde American.

'—which was just amazing! All those *jewels*! And—oh my, what a beautiful ring that is, Anton. May I look at it?'

Patiently, Anton let Kitty take his strong, elegant brown hand in both of hers. She studied the heavy gold ring on his right hand with bright blue eyes. Alex toyed with the stem of her glass, her eyes on his face. How beautiful he was, how perfect.

The light cotton shirt he wore clung to his superb torso with tailor-made closeness, and the cream-coloured lambswool jersey he had tied casually around his neck did nothing to disguise the power of his shoulders. Somehow, he was as unapproachably elegant in this summer attire as he had been in his evening clothes, and she knew that not a woman on this sunny terrace hadn't given him one long, longing stare at least.

'How *love*ly,' Kitty was saying. 'The lion of St Mark. Take a look, Alex.'

Kitty gave her a meaning nod as Alex leaned over to study the ring on Anton's hand.

It was an old, heavy seal ring. And the seal was a winged lion, poised over the world, his wings outspread.

'Weren't we just talking about that emblem?' Kitty asked, giving Alex a knowing arch of her eyebrows. 'It's very majestic.'

'It was my father's,' said Anton. He glanced up at Alex. 'I've worn it since his death. When I die, it will go to my eldest child.'

'How romantic!' Kitty bubbled.

'What a lovely day it is,' Alex sighed, leaning back in her chair. Beneath them, the long, golden beach of the Lido was bright with umbrellas and scanty bathing-costumes. She had even seen one or two women sunbathing topless, their neat little breasts tanned the same golden-brown as their long legs and slender torsos. The Lido was obviously the haunt of the Beautiful People—and with a sea the colour of lapis lazuli, and sunshine like molten gold, why not?

'The Lido is always like this in the summer,' Anton smiled, as though reading her thoughts. 'Bursting with crowds chasing the sun. And then October comes, and November, and the first mists roll in from the sea. Then the umbrellas are all furled up, and the man who rents out the deck-chairs goes home, and the Lido is suddenly deserted.'

'There must be such a wonderful social life in Venice,' said Kitty, not noticing the dry note in Anton's voice. 'My friends have all found Italian chaperones—to put it *nicely*—already. They're off, having a high old time at one of the islands. There's only me left to play gooseberry.' She fluttered her eyelashes comically at Anton, who chuckled.

'The great days of Venice have passed, I'm afraid,' he said. 'All the really rich people have gone to Rome or Milan now. The fabulous parties are few and far between these days.'

'Except the Midsummer Night's Ball,' Alex murmured.

'Yes,' nodded Kitty. 'Alex tells me you were at that last night? We saw all the hullabaloo from our *vaporetto*.'

'Ah yes, the Ball. But I'm afraid I had to come home early. My partner was suddenly indisposed.

Which reminds me,' he said, turning to Alex with bright eyes, 'that I was due to take Marina Bergatrice to the feast tonight.'

'The feast?' Kitty sparkled.

'Yes—at the Palazzo Ducale. It's a dinner-dance given every year on Midsummer Day. With a lot of tedious ceremony, I'm afraid.' He drank his Campari. 'I've just heard from Marina—she's not well enough to go.'

'I'm sorry to hear that,' said Alex quietly. She had a tingling feeling that she knew what was coming.

'The rash has gone, but she's still weak and headachy. I, on the other hand, am honour bound to attend. And I find myself short of a partner.' His smile made Alex suddenly weak. 'I wonder if I could ask you to spend a very dull evening with me, Alexandra?'

'At the feast?' She opened her mouth, then shut it. 'But I haven't anything remotely suitable——'

'That's no obstacle,' he said calmly. 'The Doge's Banquet is one of these tiresome occasions Venetians love so much—a costume ball. The atmosphere is eighteenth century. Childish, I agree,' he said urbanely, 'but sometimes amusing. I'm sure we could organise a gown for you in no time.'

Kitty looked from one to the other with sparkling eyes.

'I don't——' Alex began weakly. She was aching to say yes, aching to spend the evening with this fabulous man at a Venetian *ballo in maschera*. But——

'Oh, come on!' Kitty jogged her arm frantically. 'It sounds the most romantic thing I've ever heard! Of course you'll go!'

'I don't know what to say——'

'Then say yes,' Anton suggested, his mouth curving into an amused smile. 'And if the occasion proves too dull, then at least we can amuse one another.' The glint in his eyes contained an unmistakable message. For her alone.

'Like last night?' she suggested coolly.

'Last night I was carried away by a pair of hyacinth eyes,' he purred. 'Tonight I shall be impeccably correct.'

Kitty, who had been following this tiny bit of swordplay with eager ears, jogged Alex's elbow even more vigorously.

'For heaven's sake, Alex! You must say yes!'

'Must I?' She turned back to Anton, meeting his smile as calmly as she could. 'Very well, Signor de Cassis. If it pleases you.'

'It pleases me very much,' he said softly, his eyes holding that secret message for her again. With a lift of one eyebrow, he summoned the waiter, and ordered another round of drinks.

'While you ladies drink,' he said, rising with fluid grace, 'I'd better telephone Bettina at Castelnero, and have them bring round a selection of costumes for you to choose from. Excuse me.'

The two women watched him stride towards the bar.

'Oh my,' groaned Alex, the first chill of nervousness beginning to stir inside her, 'what have I done?'

'What a *man*!' breathed Kitty Kowalski, starry-eyed. 'What a *fabulous* man. And you're going to the Doge's Banquet with him tonight!'

'Thanks to your elbow,' Alex said reproachfully. She studied Kitty's dreamy expression with a trace of cynicism. 'So, my worldly friend,' she said gently, 'what's your considered opinion? Devil or saint?'

'Who cares?' Kitty bubbled. 'Listen, when you described Anton de Cassis to me, you didn't mention that he was as handsome as Lucifer—or built like Apollo!'

'Didn't I? Well, now you know.'

'And you're going to the banquet with him,' Kitty repeated in a trance.

'I thought you were so keen for me to watch my step?'

'That was before I met him!'

'And now you don't think I should be careful any more?'

'Listen,' said Kitty, leaning close to Alex, 'with a man like that, nobody can be careful. You're tied to his chariot wheels, kid. And whether he takes you up to heaven or drags you down to hell, my advice is—lie back and enjoy it!'

'That makes me feel a lot better,' Alex retorted. 'Oh, damn! Why did that idiot of a Princess have to eat those confounded prawns?'

'It's Fate, Alex,' Kitty grinned, and gulped at her Dubonnet. 'My God, think of all the girls who'd give an arm to be in your shoes tonight. Or in your bed!'

'That's immoral!'

'Alexis de Cassis looks immoral. Deliciously, wonderfully immoral! Believe me, just lie back and enjoy it all!'

'Thank you very much,' Alex sighed. 'You're a regular treasure-house of good, consistent advice.'

'Bettina, for God's sake tell me something about this performance tonight!'

Alex twisted round to face the little maid, who had been struggling with the catches at the back of her gown. Her hands were shaking with anxiety, and her face was pale.

'Please, *signorina*, let me attend to your dress.' Firmly, Bettina turned her round again, and tugged with nimble fingers at the rebellious fastening.

'*Madonna*, these old fashions were beautiful,' she said admiringly. 'They really knew how to dress a woman in those days——'

'Bettina! The banquet tonight—tell me what happens!'

'Why do you worry?' the Italian woman smiled. She patted the fastening, and drew Alex down on to a stool in front of the ivory dressing-table. 'Let me brush your hair now. Ah, such a colour . . .'

'What goes on there? What am I supposed to do? What——'

'The Doge's Feast is—how do you call it in English? *Un spettacolo*?'

'A pageant?'

'Exactly, a pageant. Ah, *signorina*, if only I had your hair . . .'

'Never mind my hair,' Alex interrupted. 'Just tell me what I'm supposed to do. I'm so nervous!'

'Nervous?' Bettina turned Alex's head to face the mirror, and they both stared at the reflection there. 'You have no need to be nervous, Signorina Alexandra. You will be the most beautiful woman there.'

And indeed, the dress that she and Bettina had chosen suited her more strikingly than any modern costume could have done. It was a gown of the deepest blue velvet, a colour so deep that it wasn't until Alex moved that you saw it wasn't black. The bodice hugged her waist and bust, and hinted at the fullness of her hips before flaring into a waterfall of midnight-blue folds to the ground.

'You are exquisite, *signorina*,' the maid said softly, her dark eyes appraising Alex in the mirror. 'Now, let me finish your hair, and I will tell you what I know.'

'Can't I just leave my hair down?'

'That is the fashion of the twentieth century, not the eighteenth,' Bettina smiled. 'Now, let me work—we haven't much time. At least your hair is long enough to tie up.'

'Is there dancing?'

'Of course. In the Grand Ballroom. You will be presented to the Doge—that is a great honour, *signorina*, and you must remember to kiss his hand.'

'Oh dear——'

'Keep still. There will be a lot of speeches and

ceremonies—presentations and so forth. You won't understand very much, I don't think, but that doesn't matter. And after the banquet, the rest of the evening is yours. Yours and your partner's.'

She had slipped a little pearl tiara on to the crown of Alexandra's head, and was now tying the long auburn hair across it in two sweeping wings from her temples. The pearls glowed among the lustrous hair bewitchingly.

'What sort of dances do they have?'

'All kinds,' said Bettina through a mouthful of pins. 'Waltzes, mazurkas, polkas. Pass me the velvet ribbon, *signorina*.'

'Supposing I make a fool of myself? Supposing I let Anton down?' she asked nervously, passing back the ribbon.

'You won't let him down,' Bettina smiled. She adjusted the last tendril of hair, then stood back and cocked her head to admire her handiwork. 'There. Stand up.'

Alex rose on shaky legs, and turned to face the maid. Bettina's dark eyes glowed.

'*Dio*, you look like a queen!'

She stood back, biting her lower lip in wonder. The dark blue gown set off Alex's colouring stunningly, and the swept-up Regency hairstyle emphasised the slenderness of her neck and the graceful tilt of her head. The pearls in her hair added an almost magical touch.

'Are you sure?' She tugged at her bodice fitfully. 'This dress is very décolleté——'

'When a woman has a beautiful bust, she should show it off now and then,' Bettina said practically. 'But if you insist, we can fasten it a little higher.'

'Please.'

She was braless under the soft material, and the last thing she wanted was to be too revealing on a state occasion. Bettina unfastened the fold at her breast, and pulled it closed a little higher, pinning it fast with an oval cameo brooch.

'Better?'

'Much.'

Impulsively, Bettina leaned forward to kiss Alex's cheek.

'You are very, very beautiful, *signorina*,' she whispered. 'The master's eyes will tell you that tonight. This is your wrap.' She passed the silver fur to Alex. 'There isn't much more time. I'll leave you to put on your make-up.'

With a quick squeeze of Alex's hand, she slipped out of the door.

Alex turned to the mirror, her heart in her mouth. She was incapable of perceiving her own beauty just now.

The only thought in her mind, as she applied lipstick to her full mouth with a shaking hand, was that she had come a long way, in a very short time, from that interview with Wilbert Carvel in London.

What did the evening hold for her? Disaster? Triumph?

The one thing she knew for certain was that Anton de Cassis was the most important person in her life right now. And the thought of spending a whole evening with him—and not just the thought of a fancy-dress ball with the nobility of Venice—was at the root of her stage-fright.

He still intimidated her, despite the gentleness she had seen in those grey eyes more than once now. Being with him fulfilled her so much, made her feel more alive, more fully a woman, than she had ever felt before.

Hers had been a lonely life. He had divined that, on that first magic evening together, when he said that time was standing still for them. She wasn't used to the excitement of this kind of life, wasn't accustomed to the deep thrill of being with a man like Anton.

Being brought up by a peaceful old man in a peaceful English backwater hadn't exactly prepared her for this!

And yet, though she scarcely dared to think so, he seemed to find her quietness appealing. Perhaps even alluring.

One thing was certain—she couldn't change what she was. She would never be a flirting *demi-mondaine*, a woman who commanded attention by her arrogance. Yet over the past few days, Anton had made her more aware than ever before of what she was. He had made her, in a sense, appreciate her own inner peace—now sadly ruffled!—and her innate gentleness.

And maybe, just maybe, when he was tired of the bright whirl and the flashing eyes of Venice's women, he might come to find peace in her breast.

The thought twisted her heart with a pang of mixed desire and anxiety, and she leaned forward to the mirror, chasing her secret thoughts back into their hiding-place in her heart.

A light brushing of turquoise eye-shadow made an electric contrast to the stunning colour of her eyes, and she used the faintest trace of rouge to suggest colour in cheeks she knew might be pale with nerves tonight.

She stood up, straightening the deep blue of her dress. At least she had the tall, slender figure to go with these almost imposing classical styles. She looped the silver fur around her neck, modestly covering the cream of her shoulders and breast, and gave herself one last look in the mirror.

Bettina slipped in through the door.

'The master is ready downstairs, *signorina*, and the gondola is waiting. *Dio*, you are so beautiful—but hurry, you will be late!'

Silently, Alex dabbed her favourite perfume, *Joy* at the tender hollow of her throat, and then turned to Bettina.

'I'm ready,' she said simply.

CHAPTER FOUR

IT was the most glittering occasion Alex could have visualised.

Too glittering to leave much room for nerves. She clung to Anton's arm beside one of the tall palms that flanked the great mirrors around the sides of the ballroom, and watched the dancing throngs, wide-eyed.

The ballroom was even bigger than the one at Castelnero, and consequently more imposing; but it wasn't nearly as impressive, lacking the richness of decoration, the frescoes, and above all, the Murano chandeliers.

Still, it was a fantastic and lovely sight, this vast swirl of couples, all in the graceful fashions of two centuries ago, dancing to the Viennese waltzes of a full orchestra at the far end of the hall.

'Shall we dance?'

She looked up at him eagerly. 'Oh, yes, please!'

His strong arms made a barrier for her as they swept into the crowd, and then they were spinning on the tide of the music together. Instantly, there was the unity, the oneness Alex had experienced at the Hall of Mirrors. The strength of his body was intoxicating against hers, his power guiding her, challenging her.

'You look ravishing tonight,' he said, his deep voice carrying to her above the hubbub of the crowd and the music.

'And you, *signore*, look like the prince you are,' she smiled. It was true. She had never seen him looking so masculinely beautiful. He was in a military uniform, a close-fitting black tunic that emphasised the breadth of his shoulders and the muscles in his long legs. The scarlet ribbon down the seams of his trousers and at his cuffs and throat glowed against the muted sparkle of gold piping and gold-thread embroidery. Apart from that, the black was relieved only by a supple white leather strap that crossed his torso from his left shoulder to just above his right hip.

It made him look, quite simply, magnificent. In the gondola that had brought them to the Palace, he had carried a gilt helmet with a vaguely familiar scarlet plume; and in the sparkling lobby he had left a black battle-blouse, heavy with gold braid and red ribbon.

'You carry that uniform off as though you were entitled to it,' she told him, revelling in the strength of his hand at the back of her supple waist.

'But I am entitled to it,' he grinned, spinning her around at the far end of the hall.

Dancing in this throng was like being borne on a sea of rustling satin and velvet, pearls and silk. Most of the dancers were young, their bright eyes and laughing lips expressing their excitement at this premier event; but here and there a middle-aged or elderly couple moved with stately dignity, eyes only for one another.

'Are you serious?' Alex queried.

'Certainly. This uniform is a token of my misspent youth, I'm afraid.'

'Tell me,' she pleaded, her eyes fascinated by the sexy curl of his lips.

'Not in this crowd.'

He led her out of the crush and out into one of the great vestibules, more dimly-lit and intimate, which led into the Banqueting Room.

'Champagne?'

'I'd love some.'

He kidnapped two glasses from a passing waiter, and presented one to her with a military bow.

'Your very good health, madame.'

'Thank you, *signore*,' she smiled. He took her arm,

and led her to study one of the vast banks of roses that had been arranged in the vestibules.

'Now,' she commanded, 'how do you have a right to wear this?' She stroked the supple leather strap, aware of the warmth of his chest against her fingers.

'Don't you recognise it?' His eyes were laughing at her.

'That helmet was familiar—and those white gloves. Is it some English regiment?'

'It's the Royal Horse Guards,' he grinned. 'How ignorant you are!'

'*The Horse Guards?*' Alex blinked. 'Those soldiers who——'

'Ride the white horses along Horse Guards Parade every day. Yes. They do other things besides, but no matter.' He leaned forward to take a yellow rosebud from the huge bouquet, and presented it to her with a smile that stirred something deep inside her. He wasn't even attempting to disguise the fact that he wanted her; and somehow, his unhurried gallantry made it all the more erotic for her.

'When were you in the Horse Guards?'

'For four interminable years.' He sipped champagne thoughtfully. 'My father was determined to make an English gentleman of me, my dear Alex. I went to one of the best public schools—where, surprisingly enough, I got an excellent education.' His grey eyes glinted. 'Then I wanted to go to university, become an electronics engineer. My father disagreed.'

'And your mother?'

'My mother was a beautiful butterfly. She was utterly devoted to my father. Well, he was a most lovable man. And he was determined that I should join some famous regiment, the more famous the better. And while we were still arguing the subject to and from, in the first months after I left school, he was diagnosed as having cancer of the spine.'

'Oh, how terrible,' she whispered.

'The doctors told him quite bluntly that he had only months to live. And there was no longer an argument. I knew I couldn't let him down.'

'So you joined the Horse Guards?'

'It took some doing,' he grimaced. 'You have to be very well connected to get into a regiment like that, and there was fierce competition. Being the nephew of a prince helped.'

'Did it also help being over six feet tall, and built like a Greek god?'

He stared at her, then threw his head back and laughed softly. Alex buried her confusion in a gulp of champagne, cursing her unruly tongue. The champagne and the excitement were going to her head tonight. For God's sake, she mustn't let her tongue run away with her!

'Yes,' he agreed, picking up her hand and kissing it, 'that did help.'

'How old were you?' The contact of his lips against her fingers had made the blood rise to her throat.

'Seventeen and a half—regulation age. I was nearly twenty-two when I resigned my commission. By that time both of my parents were dead—and I was so sick of the Army that I was ready to explode.'

'Did you hate it?'

'Being a Horse Guard isn't the most exciting job in the world,' he said with a reminiscent wince. 'And I wanted excitement, drama, stimulation.'

'And then?'

'Then I decided to see Europe. That's when I came to Venice for the first time, and saw Castelnero. And discovered the Venetian half of my soul.'

'Did you——'

Alex was interrupted by a fanfare of trumpets. The dancing was breaking up, and the crowds began drifting through to the Banqueting Hall.

'We'll continue the family history over dinner,'

Anton promised, tucking her hand under his arm.

Now, several of the couples had begun to greet Anton, and Alex found herself being introduced to a bewildering array of names and faces—and speculative female eyes that asked silent questions about her relationship with Anton de Cassis.

The table itself was dazzling, a thirty-foot sweep of snowy linen, crystal, silver, and white lilies. She and Anton sat together near the centre, finding themselves among a group of younger people, most of whom seemed to know Anton de Cassis well. At the far end of the table, the Doge himself sat in regal splendour.

The conversation was bewilderingly polyglot. Alex found herself answering questions in English, Italian and French, conversing in broken German with a young countess, laughing at the droll expressions of a Swiss banker.

The pressure of Anton's thigh against hers kept a glow burning inside her, and each time she glanced up at him, a quiver of pride and affection coursed through her. He was so virile, this man next to her, so strong and beautiful in his dark uniform. Between the delicious courses of the meal (roast goose and then quails on the spit) she found time to realise that Anton de Cassis was having an effect on her that might never be eradicated.

It wasn't simply that in entering his world she was encountering glamour and wealth for the first time in a quiet and modest life. It was the man himself, his bright spirit and powerful mind, that she was learning to love. As she gazed around her at the glittering guests and the sumptuous table, she knew that she would have been just as thrilled, just as dizzy with delight if she had been utterly alone with Anton de Cassis.

The golden centrepiece of the table, rising out of the banks of lilies, reminded her with a little stab how ephemeral her position was here in this company.

It was the winged lion of Venice, one conquering paw poised over a subject world.

But for the indisposition of Princess Marina Bergatrice, now languishing at home with a sick headache, she wouldn't even be here. And next year on Midsummer Day, Anton would probably be here again, with some titled beauty at his side. But not Alexandra Lacey.

What had Kitty said? Lie back and enjoy it? How could you really enjoy it, when you knew that only heartbreak and desolation awaited you at the end of the wonderful chariot ride?

'What's the matter?' Anton murmured, his eyes caressing her.

'Oh,' she said with a brittle laugh, toying with her glass, 'I just felt like Cinderella at the Ball for a moment. I'm afraid I'm not used to all this splendour.'

'You are the loveliest woman here,' he said gently. Under the table, his long, powerful fingers locked themselves in hers, sending a shiver through her body. 'Don't be overwhelmed by all this, Alex. It's only an illusion, a dream. All life is an illusion.'

'And love? Is that an illusion too?'

'To some extent.'

'Ah,' she said with a touch of bitterness, 'then all this beauty will just fade away like a dream? Is that what you think?'

His fingers bit into hers, hard enough to cause pain.

'You are real,' he said with a slow smile. 'And I am real. That is all that matters.'

'Anton,' she whispered, her heart beating fast, 'I know so little about you——'

'There is time enough to learn,' he murmured back.

'I don't know if I can trust you!'

'That you will have to learn as well,' he answered with a slow caress of her fingers in his. His thumb was brushing against the back of her hand, a warm, intimate caress that went to her senses like wine.

'You make me feel giddy,' she cried in a low voice.

'And you fascinate me,' he answered, his own voice husky. 'You fascinate me, with your violet eyes and your hair the colour of autumn! Your face is so lovely, your body like a dream that haunts me——'

'And when you've satisfied your curiosity,' she said urgently, her beautiful eyes dark, 'what then? Will you lose interest in these eyes, this body, and turn to the next challenge?'

'Don't you want me too?' he parried. 'Don't you long to touch me as I long to touch you? Don't you want to renew that kiss? Feel my arms around you?'

'*Yes*,' she shuddered. 'But I'm afraid, so afraid of your leaving me——'

'Hey, you two,' a slightly drunk young Venetian woman interrupted gaily, 'no flirting at the table! Come, Anton, tell us how the restoration at Castelnero is going.'

For a long moment, his eyes lingered on Alex's, devouring, desiring, and then, with a visible effort, he turned to the loose mouth and blurred eyes of the girl who had asked the question.

Within minutes, he had the whole table laughing at some improbable story, while Alex sat quiet, intoxicated by his presence, her emotions in a turmoil that almost frightened her.

She had never imagined that this maelstrom of passions could be possible, this inner storm that threatened to shake her foundations.

And, fleetingly, Suzie Watkins' plump, concerned face swam into her thoughts.

You are going to take care, aren't you?

Oh, Suzie, she wondered, did you have some intuition that this was going to happen to me? And what can I do?

Because God knows I'm falling in love with him. And I could no more stop myself than I could stop myself from drowning at the bottom of one of these dark Venetian canals.

Her reverie was interrupted by the commencement of the speech-making, which was to conclude the banquet. That took half an hour, and then the guests rose to enjoy the rest of the evening.

The orchestra were once more playing, and most went back to the great hall to listen, or dance if they were able.

Alex walked arm-in-arm with Anton to the staircase that led up in a grand sweep to the upper gallery. Here, from behind the marble balustrade, they were able to look down on to the scene below, out of the glare of the chandeliers.

Alex leaned forward, the marble cool against her arms, and Anton stood close beside her.

'It's so beautiful,' she murmured, watching the crowds below in fascination.

'And it all suits you very well,' he said with a warm smile. 'You fit very neatly into this fairy-tale, Alex.'

'Is it just a fairy-tale?' she asked, meeting his eyes.

'This ball? Of course. It's a beautiful illusion. I don't often attend it, I'm afraid. Usually I prefer the real world.'

'So it's all going to vanish on the stroke of midnight?' she wondered, looking out over the gay throngs. 'And all the coaches will turn into pumpkins? That's a melancholy thought.'

'Why?' he smiled. 'After all, it was only her beautiful clothes that Cinderella lost. She never lost her personal beauty, her—what shall we call it? Her real self. The Prince, after all, recognised her at once, didn't he?'

'Only after he'd tried the slipper out,' she said, her lovely mouth curving into a quiet smile. 'That always struck me as a rather odd part of the story.'

'It's an extremely polite version of what really happened,' Anton said, and there was a glint in his eyes. 'Fairy stories weren't originally intended for children, my dear Alex. All that business about seeing whether the slipper fitted was invented by Charles Perrault to replace a somewhat more earthy test in the original folk-story.' He grinned wickedly. 'Shall I tell you what the *real* test consisted of?'

'I don't think I want to hear,' she said primly, a touch of colour rising to her cheekbones. 'I like the children's version.'

'Indeed? Very revealing, Miss Lacey. Yet the adult version is no less beautiful.'

'Maybe so,' she said, uncomfortable now. She changed the subject. 'Tell me more about yourself. What happened after you came to Venice? Was that when your success began?'

'I suppose so,' he nodded. 'I'd been designing things for some years by then—more as a hobby than anything else. Sometimes one doesn't realise the potential hidden in one's hobbies. I managed to raise the capital I needed, and started Telescan. I was certain that I could make most of the telecommunications devices then in use cheaper and smaller. And more efficient.'

'And you managed?'

'Yes.'

Alex glanced at the calm face, the air of authority and self-confidence which sat so firmly on his broad shoulders.

'You're an unusual man, Signore de Cassis,' she smiled. 'Soldier, gypsy, scientist. What else?'

'And you?' he parried. 'Tell me about the young Alexandra Lacey. What was she like? Beautiful, I'm sure—but what else?'

'Very ordinary, compared to you,' she smiled. 'You just about summed it up on the night we met. I wasn't exactly a lonely child, though. Loneliness is something that's forced upon you. I chose to be on my own—a loner.' She mused, looking down into the great room below. 'Maybe that was the result of losing my parents young.'

'And your grandfather brought you up?' he prompted.

'Yes. He wasn't a rich man—and he'd retired by the time I went into his care.'

'What was he like?' Anton asked, watching her with curious eyes.

'He was a perfect gentleman,' she smiled reminiscently. 'Like you. He'd been injured in the war, and his health was never too steady, but he was full of fun—almost childlike in some things.' She laced her fingers together, leaning on her elbows. 'He was mad about kites, for example.'

'Kites?' Anton smiled.

'Yes—he was quite an expert. He used to design his own, all shapes and colours. My favourites were in the shape of fantastic birds, with beautiful plumage and streaming tails.' She looked up at him, her eyes bright with happy memories. 'There was a big stretch of heathland near where we lived, and on weekends we used to go up there with one of the kites.' She sighed. 'Those were some of the happiest times of my life. You've got no idea how high a kite can go on a good, windy day. When they were really high up, so high that you could scarcely see them, Grandpa used to let me hold the string. You'd feel it tugging against your arms like a living thing, eager to be free. It was so exhilarating! And yet,' she smiled, 'in a way it used to make me sad.'

'Why?' he asked gently.

'Because the kites were like birds—like living creatures of the air. They so wanted to be free, to sail away on the high winds! Once—and only once—I let one go.'

'What did your grandfather say?' he chuckled.

'He was very indignant,' she said with a fond smile. 'It was one of his best ones, a real beauty. He just stood, watching it fly away, with the wind ruffling his white beard, shaking his head. When I told him why I'd done it, though, he picked me up and hugged me.'

'He sounds lovely,' Anton grinned. 'And so do you. He didn't look after you all on his own, did he?'

'There was Nanny,' she told him. 'Her real name was Bridget O'Brady. Grandpa used to call her Bridie O'Brady. She was too old to be a proper nanny, and she was hampered by arthritis—but I loved her. She had a face like a Rugby forward, all cauliflower ears and flattened nose, and she could swear like a trooper when she was angry. Whenever I think of her, I see her frizzy red hair sticking out of a ridiculous old hat she used to wear.'

Anton was laughing softly at her description, his eyes merry. 'You sound like quite a family,' he suggested.

'I guess we were,' she acknowledged. 'Bridie wasn't exactly easy to live with—but she looked after me wonderfully. Grandpa couldn't pay much salary, of course, and she must have done it out of charity.'

'Or maybe love for a beautiful, lonely little girl?' he said softly. Alex looked quickly up into his eyes.

'Maybe,' she nodded softly. 'She retired when I was fourteen, and went back to Fermanagh. Then Grandpa and I were on our own again.'

'How did Grandpa cope with an adolescent girl?' Anton wanted to know. 'Tantrums and make-up, and boy-friends?'

'They were difficult years,' she admitted. 'I don't think I was as bad as some girls are—but I must have given poor old Grandpa a hell of a time. I did all the crazy things—dyed my hair green once!'

'Your beautiful hair?' he smiled, brushing the glossy curls with his hand. 'How did you have the heart?'

'Green hair was very fashionable,' she informed him.

'And there were plenty of boys?'

'Aren't there always?' she shrugged.

'Bees round a honeypot,' he said, a jealous glint in those dark grey eyes. 'Did you fall in love?'

'I didn't have the time,' she sighed. 'There was always plenty to do. I was looking after Grandpa by then—he was getting very ill. When I was seventeen, he died—and my childhood was suddenly over.'

He watched her compassionately. 'What led you into art restoring?'

'I wanted to be a dancer or a painter,' she remembered. 'I couldn't be a dancer because something happened. And like I told you, I wasn't good enough to be a painter. I went for this interview with Wilbert Carvel—and he must have seen something in me he liked.'

'I wonder what?' Anton mused ironically, touching her silky cheek with a gentle hand. She smiled.

'Well, he took me on at once, and—well, here I am.'

'You take your work seriously,' he nodded. 'That's good. And you're very skilled.'

'I'm lucky,' she shrugged. 'But you must be brilliant at your work, by the sounds of it?'

'It requires more application than inspiration,' he said. 'It's mostly hard work.'

'It sounds very glamorous.'

'It has its exciting moments,' he admitted. 'I get to see a lot of rockets launched and so on.'

'Oh—what's that like?'

Before he could reply, there was a rustle of material behind them as a couple approached. A cool voice called, 'Anton!'

They both turned to face the newcomers. The man was tall and thin, his bony face wearing a distinctly uncomfortable smile above his bow-tie, which seemed to be too tight for him.

The woman, who didn't look in the slightest uncomfortable, was a beautiful Italian. Despite the fact that her olive cheeks were pale, her full mouth and dark eyes wore a cool smile. Her glossy hair had been tied back into a pretty chignon, and at her throat, a row of diamonds glittered icily.

Her eyes drifted from Anton's face to Alex's, and then her smile widened.

'How nice to see you, Anton.' She made Alex a litle bow. 'And you, *signorina*. Anton, please introduce me to your companion.'

'Of course.' Anton's eyes were glinting as he straightened his tunic. 'Alexandra, I would like to present you to the Princess Marina Bergatrice. Her friend is Franco diMaggio, the famous couturier. Princess, may I present Alexandra Lacey, of London.'

'*Enchantee,*' the Italian woman murmured, taking Alex's hand in cool fingers.

'Princess Marina?' Alex repeated in surprise. 'But I thought you were ill with an allergy——?'

'Indeed I was,' the other said with a light laugh. 'And then I felt better, only an hour ago. Alas, by then Anton had abandoned me.' She gave him a bright smile, then turned to her companion. 'So Franco very gallantly volunteered to escort me.'

'It was no gallantry,' Franco said awkwardly, 'but a pleasure.'

'You are unpredictable, Marina,' Anton said gently.

'Did you think you had escaped me?' she laughed. Her poise and light-voiced grace were charming. It was only the coolness in those almond eyes that made the three other people in the little tableau uncomfortable.

And Alex suddenly found herself horribly embarassed, the blood rising into her cheeks as unstoppably as the dawn.

'Are you really better now?' she stammered. 'I believe seafood allergies can be very dangerous.'

'Can they?' The graceful head turned in her direction with a smile. 'Yes, I am quite better, thank you, Miss Lacey.'

'But the doctor did insist you took it easy, Marina,' Franco diMaggio put in nervously, tugging at his tie.

'Ah, but I so wanted to see Anton in his uniform,' the Princess said in her light voice. She gave Anton a lingering look, taking him in from head to toe, then turned again to Alex. 'And I wanted to see the charming English lady that everyone's been telling me about.' She studied Alex thoughtfully, then looked back at Anton. 'Indeed, you make a very handsome couple. You are so dashing in that uniform, Anton.'

'Thank you,' Anton smiled. He seemed utterly unperturbed by the turn events had taken—unlike Alex, who was ready to melt with mortification. Why on earth had this woman chosen to come, after all? To humiliate her?

The Princess was undeniably attractive. Her almond eyes, intriguingly slanted in a high-cheekboned face, were bright with intelligence. The smiling mouth, wide and rather narrow-lipped, was elegantly sexy. And now that smile was turned full on to Anton.

'I seem to have missed dinner,' she was saying.

'I would have saved you a goose-leg if I'd known you were coming,' Anton told her. 'Are you hungry?'

'Famished. I haven't eaten a thing since those abominable prawns.' She cocked her head winningly at the two men. 'Darling Anton, wouldn't you try and find me something to nibble at? A bit of fruit would be so welcome. And Franco, my sweet—a little glass of champagne?'

'But the doctor——'

'Damn the doctor,' Marina purred, her eyes bright. 'And in the meantime we ladies will powder our faces, n'est-ce pas?'

'Marina——' Anton began gently.

'I'm not going to eat your partner, Anton,' she interrupted.

'No? I've heard it said that Venetian ladies are cannibals,' he said with an arch of one dark eyebrow.

'And I've heard it said that soldiers are faithless,' she rejoined smoothly. 'But I don't believe it. If you don't go, Anton caro, poor Franco will get lost.'

Anton's eyes met Alex's for a second, and then he

nodded slightly. 'Very well, Marina. Come on, diMaggio—and on the way I'll introduce you to some prospective customers.'

The two men walked away, leaving Alex, her heart thudding uncomfortably, with the Princess. Silently, they watched the two men going down the marble staircase.

'He is very handsome, isn't he?' Marina said softly.

'Very,' Alex agreed. The Italian woman turned her bright, cool eyes on to Alex.

'And you are very lovely. They said you were. That colouring is very striking—and you have excellent bones.'

Alex had the unpleasant feeling that the Princess would have liked to gnaw them; but the smile with which it was said was warm enough.

'You're kind to say so.'

'Oh no—merely sincere. Shall we walk along the balcony a little?'

Marina Bergatrice was slightly shorter than Alex, but she moved with a lithe grace. As they strolled along the plush carpet, to all intents and purposes a pair of friends enjoying a confidence, Alex cleared her throat.

'I'm afraid this is a somewhat embarrassing situation, Princess——'

'Embarrassing? Not at all.'

'But I've taken your place, so to speak.'

'I hope you haven't taken my place altogether,' the Italian woman said gently, and the glitter in those almond eyes was as cold as a pair of rapiers. Alex remembered with an inward grimace what Bettina had told her: *she and Signor de Cassis make such a wonderful couple—I am sure they will be married soon.*

'Besides,' Marina was continuing, 'I had no intention of coming. I assumed that Anton would take Sara Fallaci, or some dull creature of that sort.'

'Am I not a dull creature?' Alex smiled.

'You? No, Miss Lacey, you aren't even remotely

dull.' The smile was smooth, charming. 'Which is why I've dragged myself out of bed to take a look at you.'

'You did?' Alex rejoined with a sinking heart.

'Of course. News travels so quickly in this Venice of ours—and there were literally dozens of my friends eager to bring me the news that Anton had come with the beautiful English girl from London.' Now there was something sharp in that smile.

'Well,' Alex said calmly, 'now you've taken a look at me.'

'Yes. It's as well never to underestimate the opposition,' the other woman replied.

'I wasn't aware that there was a war on,' said Alex with raised eyebrows.

'Oh, there is now,' Marina replied. She cocked her head aside on her slender neck and studied Alex. The exchange of glances was brief and cold. 'Anton is far too fond of you, Miss Lacey.'

'Fond?' Alex challenged. 'We've barely met, Princess!'

'For a couple who've barely met, Miss Lacey, you are *far* too fond of one another.'

'And what makes you say that?'

'My maid is married to Bettina Rossi's brother,' Marina explained. 'Bettina is the pretty little maid at Castelnero.'

'I see,' Alex said slowly.

'Maids talk.'

'What do they say?'

'They say,' the Princess replied with one of her light smiles, 'that Anton was kissing you in the Hall of Mirrors on the night you arrived in Venice.'

Alex's cheeks flushed red and angry, and she clenched her teeth to keep back the retort that was at the tip of her tongue. Marina Bergatrice's mouth expressed distaste.

'I dislike this tittle-tattle as much as you.'

'Why do you repeat it, then?'

'Because I intend to marry Anton de Cassis,' came the low reply. 'And I do not intend to let any redheaded sexpot get in my way.'

'I prefer your poison to your honey,' snapped Alex, strangely undaunted by the fierce expression suddenly in the Princess' eyes. 'At least you are frank now.'

'My concern,' the other shrugged, 'is for you as much as for my own stake.'

'How kind!'

'Anton is a prince, Miss Lacey. You are a nobody. A pretty nobody—but a nobody all the same. Do you really imagine that Anton has any interest in you beyond that youthful body of yours?'

'Does Anton know that you intend to marry him?' Alex said after a pause.

'He will do. When I choose it.'

'How subtle you must be,' Alex gritted.

'Venetians are subtle. My family have ruled in Venice for three hundred years, *Miss* Lacey. I am a princess. Anton is a prince. We were made for each other—it's as simple as that.'

'Is this what you came here to tell me?' Alex said in a tense voice, biting back the retort that the other woman's cruel words had provoked inside her.

'Exactly,' the Princess nodded. She watched Alex from under lowered lashes, her sexy smile firmly in place. For all the emotion she showed, they might as well have been discussing the weather. 'Stay away from Anton de Cassis, little painter's apprentice. He is mine.'

'Anton—yours?' For the first time, Alex laughed softly. 'You're making a big mistake, Marina.'

'Why so?' came the cold reply.

'Anton de Cassis belongs to no woman.'

'Nonsense! The man was made for love and woman's pleasure.'

'He was made for himself,' Alex corrected. 'One day he will love. He will love whom he chooses, on his own terms. And neither you nor I will have the slightest choice as to who that will be. It will most likely be neither of us.'

'You think so?' Marina's smile was scournful. 'You don't know me, Miss Lacey. Nor do you know Anton. He is a Venetian, like me.'

'He is an Englishman, like *me*,' Alex retorted. 'He was born in England, bred in England.'

'His father was the brother of a prince!'

'His mother was an English actress!'

'I don't intend to bandy arguments with you,' said Marina, her arching brows now drawn down in undisguised anger. 'I've warned you to stay away from Anton. Better still, go back to London at once, and never come back.'

The two women stared at each other with the quiet anger of two beautiful lionesses measuring one another for the fray. Then Alex broke the silence.

'Princess Marina, I'm afraid your aristocratic lineage doesn't impress me. There were Laceys in England during the Crusades, and Laceys in the Civil War. Your so-called aristocracy is degenerating, sinking into the sea—just as Venice is sinking.'

'How dare you!'

'How dare you try and bully me?' Alex retorted. 'If you have such pretensions to noble birth, why don't you start living up to them? I refuse to be bludgeoned, Princess—and in any case, I don't believe that so-called breeding has anything to do with love.'

'Love?' Marina Bergatrice laughed harshly, her lovely face now distorted with passion. 'You think a creature like you—barely twenty, all smiles and legs—could arouse love in Anton de Cassis?'

'Why should he love you, in that case?' Alex rejoined.

'I don't ask him to love me,' she snarled. 'I want him to marry me.'

'Then I wish you the best of luck,' Alex said quietly.

Stung beyond endurance, the Princess's face darkened.

'Let me tell you something,' she hissed, 'little upstart! Anton de Cassis was in my bed and in my arms before you ever heard the name of Castelnero!'

There was a deathly silence. A taut smile stretched itself across Marina's lips, and she raised a hand slowly, and snapped her fingers at Alex. 'What now, English virgin?'

In the silence, Anton and Franco diMaggio approached, carrying a tray of champagne glasses. As they arrived, Anton's eyes took in the white faces of the two women.

'Alex? What's the matter? Are you ill?'

'Yes,' Alex snapped, 'I'm sick to my heart. I'm going home.' She stalked to the marble stairs, oblivious of the curious stares people were giving her. Anton's eyes were like thunder as he strode after her.

Silently, she allowed him to help her out of the gondola on to the steps of Castelnero. The water lapped softly against the ancient stonework.

She hadn't cried, at least.

Anton's arm was strong around her as they walked through the door and into the echoing hallway. He took the fur wrap from her, and tugged off his gloves.

'What did she say to you?' he asked quietly.

'That——' She stopped herself.

'What did she say?' he asked again. 'Did she insult you?'

'She tried to,' Alex smiled bitterly.

Anton's eyes were grave.

'I'm sorry this evening ended so badly for you, Alexandra. I didn't expect this to happen.'

'It was nothing,' she said, her voice brittle and shaky. She reached up and pulled the pearl tiara out of her hair with a wrench, oblivious to the pain. The thick tresses tumbled down around her face, and she brushed them back roughly with her fingers.

Anton took her arm firmly and gently.

'Did you know there was a full moon tonight?' he asked conversationally.

'I didn't notice.'

'Come into the courtyard.'

'I'd rather go to bed——'

'Come,' he commanded, and Alex let him lead her through the beautiful rooms, feeling as though her heart would break.

A set of wide French doors led unexpectedly out into a courtyard, paved with smooth-worn stones, and silent as the tomb. Palms grew in great stone tubs all around, and there was a pot-garden, redolent of herbs and aromatic plants, arranged down the stairs.

Anton led her under a great trailing creeper that swept down from the balconies above, and into the peace of this alcove.

'Living in Venice means living with the sea,' he said calmly. 'This courtyard is here to remind us of the land, of plants and earth and flowers.'

It was a beautiful, serene place; in the day, it would be deliciously cool and shaded by the palms, and the stones would be refreshingly cold under hot, bare feet. Now, in the Venetian moonlight, it was a magical place, patterned with shadows and pearly light. Despite herself, Alex felt its spell stealing over her.

'Look,' he pointed. She stared up into the moon, a huge golden pearl in the sky above, a sky as dark as the blue of her dress. Anton's body was close to hers, and she could feel his warmth against her skin.

'Now,' he said, his voice commanding, 'what did Marina say to you?'

'That she was going to marry you,' she answered dully.

'What else?'

'Nothing else.'

'Alex.' His voice, soft as it was, cut like a lash. 'Don't ever lie to me. What else did she say?'

'That all you wanted was my body,' she said, a catch in her voice. 'That you and she—had—had slept together——'

'And you believed her?'

'Do you deny it?' she challenged, a rising note of anger in her voice.

In the moonlight, his eyes were fathomless.

'Would you believe me if I did deny it?' he asked softly.

'Of course not,' she retorted. 'But I'd like to hear you say it, all the same. I'd like to see the great Anton de Cassis reduced to lies to get his way with a cheap little foreigner——'

'Alexandra, stop it!' he cut through her bitterness.

'Why should I? You've played me for a fool, Anton. Damn you,' she said in a shaky voice, 'why did you have to do this to me?'

'Do what?' he asked quietly.

'If you wanted to take me to bed, why didn't you just do it? Why didn't you just take me?' She faced him with blazing eyes. 'You didn't have to ensnare me with all that—that—romantic rubbish. You didn't have to break my heart!'

'Do I mean that much to you?' he asked, his voice gentle.

'You don't mean a damn thing to me,' she snarled. 'As for all that pageantry and pretence at the banquet tonight—you can keep it! I'm not fooled any more. You don't mean a thing to me!'

'Don't I?'

'No!'

He reached out, spreading his fingers luxuriously through her tumbled hair, and drew her face to him. The passionate curve of his lips descended on to hers.

'You're wrong,' he whispered, his breath warm on her mouth. 'You're very wrong, my sweet love.'

CHAPTER FIVE

'LET me go!' she hissed, her fingers digging into his sinewy wrists. Her mind was still full of the bitter things she wanted to say to him, but he was too strong, and as he kissed her full on the lips, she could only dig her nails into the hard muscles of his arms in a futile attempt to hurt him.

His kiss was harsh, a brief, male caress that shocked her with the force of its passion. They stared into one another's eyes, rigid.

'Anton,' she commanded shakily, 'let me go!'

'Not yet,' he smiled, his eyes warm on hers. 'You're so desirable, my darling Alex, so very lovely . . .'

This time he kissed with a deliberate, clinging sensuality. His hands slid down her neck, across her bare shoulders, and down her sides, a caress that seemed to burn like red coals through the velvet of her dress.

Something responded inside Alex at that moment, a hard jolt of electricity that quivered down her belly to her loins, making her shudder against him. She knew that he had felt it in her, had shared it, and now his kiss became an exquisitely erotic exploration that swelled her pulses and set them racing. His mouth was a sweet torment that knew no shame, that stopped at nothing beyond the naked desire to arouse her and make her his—an exploration so shockingly intimate that her very bones seemed to be melting.

'Please,' she gasped, 'don't do this to me!'

'Why not? This is what you do to me, Alex. Except that you don't have to touch me to do it.'

He buried his face against the satiny skin of her throat, his mouth parted against her warm flesh as though he wanted to drink the very taste and smell of her. Shuddering, she arched her neck in a tormented ecstasy.

'You smell like warm honey,' he murmured, kissing the tender underside of her jawline, following the beautiful curves to her ear.

'I don't want this,' she pleaded, her fingers trembling on the pulsing strength of his arms, feebly pushing at him.

'But you do.' His breath was warm in her ear, a thrilling whisper that reached deep into her mind, finding the truth there. His hands brushed the curve of her hips, tracing the perfection of her figure under the soft material of her dress. Her eyes fluttered closed, and he smiled down at the dewy face beneath him. He kissed the long lashes that lay languidly over the violet eyes.

'This is how you looked when I put you to bed that first night, Alex. So innocent, so desirable. I wanted you then, and I want you now. I want you very much.'

His last words were only a whisper. His kiss stole softly upon her unresisting lips, melting her will; his tongue brushed against her mouth, a flame that set the sensitive skin ablaze, challenging it to respond.

She scarcely knew that her own arms had crept around his neck, or that her fingers were lost in the dark curls of his hair.

The moon poured its pure, pearly light into the silent courtyard. The faintest hint of a warm breeze was stirring the palm-leaves, dappling the paving-stones below with a criss-cross of trembling shadow.

And beside the rustling creeper, whose scented petals dropped from time to time on to the worn stones, the perfect image of two lovers, clinging to one another, lost in a kiss that for one burning minute was touching eternity.

Except that there would be no eternity of love for Alex.

Of that she was certain. In her heart she had always borne the warning thought that this bliss might not last. And now, in the aftermath of the ball, her mind and heart were overshadowed with forebodings.

In his uniform tonight, Anton had been so dazzling—like a prince from a fairytale. And, like a fairytale, this reality was too good to be true. Princess Marina had been right. How could she, a shy, reserved woman, whose beauty lay in her tranquillity and gentleness, hope to keep a man like Anton? Anton, who was so vivid, so burning with life and strength, so alive with poised, concentrated energy. Anton, who was all the things she was not. It couldn't be!

'Anton, please let me go,' she said in a low voice, resting her hot forehead against his shoulder. 'I want to go to bed now.'

'Not unless I can come with you,' he answered huskily.

'Why are you doing this?' she cried shakily. 'Do you want to be cruel to me, to humiliate me? Or are you just incapable of resisting the lure of the chase?'

'Doesn't it occur to you that I might simply want you?' he asked gently. One hand pressed her to him, and he lifted the other to touch the cameo brooch that secured the bodice of her dress.

'There's no such thing as simple desire. It all has to be paid for some time, Anton——'

'You're shaking,' he said quietly. 'Your body contradicts your words, Alex.'

With a little click, the brooch's pin slipped open, and it dropped on to the stones with a tiny clatter.

'No!'

'Why do you fight it?' His fingers eased the velvet aside as she arched her neck back, shuddering.

'Because this is just a game to you! Because——'

'Because you're afraid.'

His fingers caressed the naked, taut swell of her breasts, finding the ultra-sensitive rosebud peaks.

Trembling, she clung to his arms, her whole body racked by feelings she had never imagined, could never have anticipated were possible.

He cupped her breasts in warm hands, her nipples thrusting their message of desire and welcome into his palms, as their lips touched.

Now there seemed to be some fine electricity that leaped between them. Her lips were dry and hot as they brushed against his, and the contact of his mouth was like rain on parched earth. He kissed her slowly, deliberately slowly, as his hands gently massaged the smooth, sensual curves of her breasts.

No one had ever touched her like this, made her feel even a shadow of what Anton was making her feel. It was as though she were fusing with him, the ecstasy and torment of his touch actually welding his flesh to hers, making them one creature, one mind, one soul. The tension had drained from her muscles, leaving her as powerless as a kitten under its master's caress, as though her body were changing into liquid, as though her blood were molten honey.

'Yes,' she whispered, 'I am afraid. I'm afraid of this, Anton, of what you do to me.'

'What do I do to you?' His fingers teased the coral-pink peaks of her breasts to even harder buds of desire, making her moan. 'Tell me!'

'You bewitch me!'

'And you bewitch me, little sorceress!' He kissed her hard, crushing her lips beneath his. 'Since I saw you, I've thought of nothing but you, Alexandra Lacey! You possess my thoughts, my dreams, my desires——'

His voice throbbed with passion, and she could feel his need for her, potent and intoxicating, thrusting against her body, shamelessly taut in the thrust of his hips.

With a huge effort of will, she twisted her mouth away from his and stepped back, pulling the blue velvet closed over her naked breasts. The soft material seemed as rough as sackcloth against her aroused nipples.

Anton was a tall, dark figure in front of her, his brows lowering over smoky eyes.

'You are determined to make me burn for you, then?' he growled, the first hint of anger in that deep, caressing voice.

'If it's any consolation,' she said in a quivering voice, 'I shall be burning for you, Anton.'

'But, my darling——' he stepped up to her, his arms reaching for her, 'the answer is so simple.'

'I can't accept that answer,' she whispered. Her head seemed too heavy to lift, and her neck drooped, her long auburn hair trailing in front of her face. 'I'm not available like this, not ever.'

'You don't know what I feel for you,' he said grimly, powerful fingers biting into her shoulders.

'I know,' she retorted in a low voice. 'I know exactly how you feel. I'm the peasant girl, and you're the lord of the Manor, determined to have his pleasure——'

'You dishonour yourself to talk like that!'

'You dishonour me,' she replied. Her voice rang soft and clear round the moonlit courtyard. The wind had risen slightly, and a quick scud of clouds passed in front of the moon. The momentary darkness sealed their separation.

'Is this the result of what Marina said to you?' he asked quietly. Alex shook her long hair back, and looked up at the moon through blurred eyes. Another cloud darkened its brightness for a moment.

'Marina was only protecting her interests,' she answered. 'But what she said brought home to me what I'd already found out in my heart.'

'And what was that?'

'That you could never be serious about me.' She met his dark gaze, then dropped her long lashes. 'That

I might satisfy you for a night, or even a year of nights—but that, in the end, I wouldn't be enough for you.'

'How, "enough"?' he asked, his tone bitter.

'I'm not a princess, like Marina, or like all those dozens of other beauties at the banquet tonight——'

'God! Do you think I give a damn about that?' he snarled.

'I can't take that chance,' she said, close to tears.

'Chance? Doesn't it occur to you that I'm taking a chance with *you*, Alex?'

'What have you to fear from me?' she rejoined with a laugh that was almost a sob. 'You, who are so strong, so sure of yourself! You're like that winged lion these Venetians are so fond of—a born conqueror. Well, this is one little world that refuses to be conquered!'

She turned from him to hide the tears that were spilling between her eyelids, and ran back into the house.

'Alex!'

Unheeding, she fled up the marble stairs, not pausing till she was safe in her ivory suite. The exquisite calm of the room seemed to mock her passion as she turned the key in the lock, and leaned against the door, sobbing.

In the courtyard, the moonlight had faded. The first heavy drops of summer rain had begun to splash on to the paving-stones, as warm as tears. They knocked the flimsy petals from the creeper and battered them against the ground. They splashed dark spots on to the dark tunic of the man who stood there, his eyes angry and unseeing, one fist clenched in a gesture of anger and frustration.

When Bettina brought Alex's breakfast in the next morning, her dark eyes were alight with mischief.

'The melon is very sweet, Signorina Alexandra,' she

invited, placing the green semi-circle in front of Alex.
'You will enjoy it.'

'Thanks,' she said dully.

'The Signorina must be tired after her wonderful
night,' Bettina beamed. 'Oh, I almost forgot.' She
reached into her pocket, and held something out to
Alex. 'I found this in the courtyard. You must have
mislaid it.'

It was the oval cameo brooch that had fastened the
breast of her gown. At the sight of it, her stomach
contracted with a hard tug of remembered desire, to
be replaced almost at once by a wave of misery. She
looked up at Bettina. By the maid's smile, she
obviously thought Alex and her master had spent the
night making passionate love.

Slowly she reached out and took the brooch.

'Bettina—I understand your brother is married to
Princess Marina's personal maid?'

'That is right, *signorina*,' she agreed.

'Tell me something—did you see Signor de Cassis
kiss me in the hall of Mirrors, on the night I arrived
here?'

A dusky flush rose above Bettina's smile.

'Yes, Signorina Alexandra,' she whispered.

'And you told your sister-in-law?'

'Yes, *signorina*.' Suddenly her eyes widened in
dismay. 'Have I done something wrong?'

Alex sighed. 'I'm afraid your sister-in-law went
straight to the Princess. And the Princess,' she
grimaced, 'was not pleased.'

'Oh, *signorina*!' Bettina bit her knuckles in horror.
'That stupid Carla! I made her swear not to say
anything!'

'Perhaps Marina wormed it out of her,' said Alex
with a little shrug.

'I am so sorry, *signorina*, so very sorry——'

'Don't be—it's all over and done with now. But that
wasn't what I wanted to talk to you about.' Alex

pushed the slice of melon aside. 'Bettina, that kiss you saw Anton—I mean, Signor de Cassis give me. It meant nothing, you understand?'

'But——'

'Nothing. There's no romance between us.'

'Oh, *signorina!*' Bettina's face was stricken. 'Have you quarrelled because of my foolishness?'

'No,' Alex said firmly. 'There was nothing between us in the first place. When Anton kissed me that night, he meant nothing. Is that clear?'

'A man does not kiss a woman like that if he means nothing by it, *signorina*.'

'Bettina——'

'Signorina Alexandra,' the maid said, 'I have made a foolish mistake in telling Carla your secrets. I promise that. And believe me, I will safeguard your secrets with my life from now on!'

'I don't have any secrets,' Alex smiled.

'You see, *signorina*,' Bettina went on, unheeding, 'I had no idea that things were serious between you and the master.'

'But they aren't——'

'I thought it was merely a—what do you say—a flirtation?' Bettina took Alex's hand earnestly. 'Now that I know how things stand, I will be more serious, I swear it!'

'But things *aren't* serious between me and Anton,' Alex protested in frustration. 'You've got it all wrong!'

'*Signorina*,' Bettina sat down on the bed, her dark face sincere, 'I am a woman, like you. You could not hide such a thing from me if you tried. I know how you feel about the master.' She smiled gravely. 'Can you deny it now?'

Alex looked away. 'I thought you were so keen for Anton to marry Marina Bergatrice, anyway?' she said obliquely.

'It was what I expected,' the Italian girl said quietly, 'but not what I wished. The Principessa Bergatrice is very beautiful, very rich. She would bring our master much honour.' She smiled, tilting her head at Alex. 'But she is not like you, Signorina Alexandra. She is arrogant, that one, arrogant and full of vanity. My sister-in-law tells me many things about her—things I do not like. She would not make Signor de Cassis happy, never in a thousand years. Not the way you could.'

'Me?' Alex blinked.

'Of course,' Bettina smiled. 'Anyone can see that the blood runs warm in your veins. Marina is like ice. You are like fire, *signorina*, quick and light. You could keep a man contented in bed.'

'Bettina!' Alex's mouth creased in a smile despite herself. 'You mustn't say such things!'

'Why not? It's the truth.' The dark eyes sparkled. 'And the master—he is a real man, *signorina*. You will never find such another.' She sighed, shaking her head. '*Madonna*, what a man he is! He has helped my family countless times. He paid for my sister's teeth and my father's operation. He is an angel.'

'I believe you,' Alex nodded, suppressing laughter. 'But I don't think your master is really interested in me, Bettina.'

'Ah, no?' Bettina threw back her head to laugh. She picked up the cameo brooch, and held it up with a grin. 'Then why did he take this from your bosom?' Alex coloured as Bettina's eyes dropped to where her breasts were making soft peaks against her nightdress. 'You are beautiful, Signorina Alexandra, and you are desirable—very desirable. If you think Signor de Cassis does not want you, then you are deceiving only yourself.'

'Physical desire is one thing,' Alex said wryly. 'True emotion is quite another.'

'And you think Anton de Cassis is not true?' Bettina threw her hands up in scorn. 'He is as true as steel, as true as the sun! Do you think he would not walk through the fire for you if he really wanted you?'

'But that's just it—*does* he really want me?' Alex demanded.

Bettina stared at her, then shook her dark head slowly.

'If you don't know for yourself, *signorina*, no one can tell you.' She smiled, showing beautiful white teeth. 'You will learn, in time. Now, I shall leave you to your melon. It is very sweet, *signorina*, but not as sweet as love. And from now on, I will guard your secrets with my life.' With a conspiratorial nod, Bettina let herself out.

Alex sat for a long moment, thinking hard. Then, smiling slightly, she turned to her melon.

Bettina had been right. It was remarkably sweet.

She rose, stretching luxuriously. Her breasts felt tender, as though Anton's caress had seared them, but a deep joy at being alive was somehow running through her veins.

She dressed in a light, plain linen dress with a wide collar and short sleeves. Businesslike wear. Wanting to feel free, she wore neither tights nor bra, only a plain pair of cotton briefs under the cool dress; and slipping sandals on her feet, stepped out of her suite to do battle with the ravages of time on ancient oil paint.

It was a rainy day. The beautiful view from the high windows of Castelnero was grey and rain-washed. In the summer drizzle, gondolas plied the canals with sleek black haste. All the business of the city was carried out by the waterways, Alex had discovered. In the intervals between her work, she watched the traffic below. Besides the gondolas and *vaporetti*, little barges trudged up and down selling fruit and vegetables, fresh fish, or carrying loads of cement or bricks.

The police used efficient-looking motorboats, mail came in red-and-grey speedboats, and once she even saw a funeral pass by, the flower-heaped coffin on an ornate gilt-and-black launch, the mourners following in decent placidity in gondolas behind. It was a

strange but orderly world, this city whose streets were
canals.

That morning she finished the portrait of Ginestra
de Cassis, and cleaned several smaller, easier canvases.
She was cataloguing the paintings as she went, adding
little notes about the identities of the artists when no
signature was visible, making estimates of the age and
probable value of the works.

It was work she excelled in, and not even the jolting
memories of last night which returned unbidden to
mind now and again could disturb her rhythm for
long.

Anton did not return for lunch.

As she ate alone in the great dining-room, Alex
wasn't sure whether she was relieved or glad. There
was an ache in her for him, an unsatisfied emptiness
that hurt whenever she thought of him. Which was all
the time.

There was so much she wanted to say to him, to try
and explain why she had behaved as she had. To try
and repair the rift between them. Yet she knew it
might be better to say nothing at all. Anton was a man
of powerful passions, and she knew that what she
had said last night had hurt and angered him.
Perhaps the best thing would be not to go near him
again. Ever.

She had said she might go down to the YWCA in
the afternoon to meet Kitty Kowalski; but somehow
she couldn't face Kitty's eager questions and prying
now.

She worked through the afternoon, moving from
one room to another, setting aside the paintings that
were in need of her assistance, making notes of those
that didn't. Most of the rooms on that floor were
bedrooms, their beauty and grandeur silent and
unoccupied.

But the last one she went into, at the far end of the
corridor, wasn't disused. As soon as she had stepped

through on to the thick dove-grey carpet, she knew whose suite this was.

She had no doubt that Anton de Cassis had had this suite decorated specifically to suit his taste. His personality was evident in every line of the stunning ebony and hide furniture, in the maroon wallpaper, in the slightly barbaric spendour of the Berber rugs.

Silently, Alex walked through to the bedroom, her eyes taking in the huge, beautiful landscape that covered one section of the walls between the heavy curtains.

The bedroom made her gasp quietly. It contained little more than a bed—but what a bed! The four-poster was so huge that Alex was sure sheets and quilts for it would have to be made by hand. From the towering ebony posts, a heavy swathe of some Oriental material swung down among thick golden rope with embroidered tassles. The canopy was an exquisite, shimmering Afghan silk, and the bedspread was a sea of scarlet-and-black stitched calico flowers.

The bed gave the impression of an almost savage spendour, like the tent of some Bedouin sheikh, or the palanquin of an Eastern emperor. Even the pillows and cushions liberally spread over the quilt were ablaze with Oriental colours and patterns, glowing with velvet and watered silk.

Alex gaped at it, then slowly gazed round the remainder of the room. There was almost nothing else to detract from the affairs of the bedchamber—no telephone, no television, no extraneous furniture. Just a scattering of huge cushions on the carpet, which was so luxuriously thick as to silence every footfall.

The walls and ceiling had been covered with a deep scarlet silk. The only lighting apparent was the standard lamp near the bed, a beautiful Venetian Renaissance piece of a little naked Moor holding up a flambeau.

So this was Anton de Cassis' bedroom? Fascinated,

Alex padded through to the bathroom, and pushed open the door. The same deep scarlet was carried through into the Florentine tiles on floor and ceiling of the bathroom. The bath, like hers, was sunk into the floor, an octagon of red onyx. Where in her bathroom a faun peeped through the trailing pelargonium, here there was a full-length nude in black marble—a breathtakingly beautiful sculpture of a woman, her arms upraised, her full breasts straining as she threw back her head to let her hair unfurl in thick waves down her back.

The whole ensemble was stunningly sensuous—and almost Spartan in its neatness. This was the suite of a man who loved beauty and exotic magnificence, but who was no hedonist. These were the chambers of a man whose mind was icily ordered. A man who could balance his desires and pleasures with an iron self-control.

There were no clothes thrown carelessly around, no confusion of personal possessions. Guiltily, Alex recalled the slight disorder in her own suite. And what personal possessions were visible, were all clearly chosen with an unerring and positive taste.

The only bottle visible on the shelf was a flaçon of Schiaparelli aftershave. Lying on a chair was a microcomputer chess game, its screen glowing with red digits and letters. She picked it up carefully, and glanced at the label: Telescan.

Putting it back, she walked through into the bedroom again, pausing in front of that astonishingly beautiful bed.

What would it be like to lie there, under that shimmering silk, in Anton's arms? The tautening of her stomach at the thought was her own answer. Slowly, as though hypnotised by the barbaric magnificence, she walked towards it, and without thinking, crawled into the middle and lay back with a sigh. The mattress was firm, comfortable.

'Anton,' she whispered, and stretched out her arms and legs like a languid cat, arching her neck . . .

And slowly, the realisation dawned on her that Alexandra Lacey was never going to be the same again. In these brief days, something inside her had changed for ever—as though the act of falling in love had forced her through the last shreds of her adolescence, into full womanhood.

She gazed up at the silk canopy above with hazy violet eyes, her long, rich hair tumbled around her head like streamers of fire. Wasn't it useless to fight her love for him? It was an emotion of such power inside her, capable of plunging her into despair or lifting her into ecstasy.

Why shouldn't she just let herself go—trust Anton? After all, wasn't it just possible that his interest in her might go beyond pure sex, that he might feel something of the emotions she felt for him?

A wry smile tugged at her beautiful mouth.

'You shouldn't try and fool yourself, Alex,' she whispered. No, she couldn't get out of it so easily. If she was going to let Anton have his way with her, then she must do so on his terms. She had said exactly that to Marina Bergatrice.

And this emotion inside her was older and deeper than any morality. Why should she cling hypocritically to an outmoded convention? The real reason she hadn't given way to Anton long before this was that she was afraid of being hurt by him.

Because she was afraid he would turn out like Barry Dent. That he would do what Barry had done to her, that night in the car. Barry had taught her to beware of men, hadn't he? She had at least that to be grateful for.

And that was why she couldn't cope with Anton's potent sexuality. Blame Barry Dent for that. Simple.

Well, no—there was more to it than that.

Oh, Granddad, why did you bring me up such a

little Puritan? Why couldn't you have been one of those free and easy foster-parents who tell their kids to go out and try everything? You didn't have to burden me with this Victorian conscience about sex!

The sound of the outer door clicking open disturbed her reverie.

Panic-stricken, she shot upright in the bed, her heart in her mouth. Someone was in the drawing-room! Anton? She caught the murmur of a deep voice, and knew it was his.

Triple damn! Desperately, she looked around the bedroom. There was nowhere to hide—and in any case, what a ridiculous, farcical thing that would be to do.

But her situation wasn't farcical. If Anton found her here, he would think——

Slowly, she lay back down on the intricate cover, her mind meshing into a fatal decision.

Let him find her here.

Hadn't she just been deciding whether or not to embark on an affair with Anton de Cassis? Well, destiny had taken a hand now. Let him find her here, let him take her, any way he wanted to. The long struggle was over. With painfully beating heart, she closed her eyes again, and waited for the bedroom door to open.

It did almost at once. Alex lay motionless, waiting in an agony of suspense, in the endless pause which followed.

But the cool, light voice which broke the silence was not Anton de Cassis'.

'Anton,' said the Princess Marina Bergatrice, her beautiful almond eyes like chips of black ice, 'you appear to have a visitor.'

CHAPTER SIX

NUMB with horror. Alex sat up.

Marina Bergatrice's beautiful face was set with fury, the sable fur that was wrapped around her seeming to crackle with electricity like a cat's coat. She turned to face Anton, who walked into the bedroom with an enquiring lift to his dark brows, a heavy camelhair overcoat half off his broad shoulders. As his deep grey eyes met Alex's, he paused for an instant. They stared at one another in mutual astonishment, then Anton's eyebrows lowered dangerously. He pulled the coat off and laid it aside.

For a moment, nobody spoke. Then Marina broke the silence.

'I seem to have disrupted your arrangements, my dear Anton,' she said with barely-suppressed fury. 'Or did you mix your appointments up?'

'I had no appointment with Miss Lacey,' Anton growled. 'What are you doing here, Alex?'

The blood that had drained from her face now returned in a hot flood. Oh God, she thought bitterly, you fool, you complete *fool*! While she had been lying here, dreaming that Anton might be in love with her, he had been on his way here with Marina Bergatrice— an assignation that was to end in this bed.

Filled with disgust and self-anger, she slid to her feet.

'I came in here to look at the paintings,' she said in a low voice. 'I didn't mean to interrupt your evening. If you'll excuse me, I'll go now.'

'Not so fast, little vixen!' Marina stepped in front of Alex, her face still furious. 'I want some kind of explanation from you, Miss Lacey!'

'Miss Lacey doesn't have to give you any explanations, Marina,' Anton said calmly. 'This is my house.'

'Do you take me for a fool, Anton?' Marina spun round on him with glittering eyes. 'Do you think I don't know that you and this child have been having an affair under my very nose?'

'That's a lie!' Alex burst out.

'All Venice knows it,' Marina sneered.

'Control yourself,' Anton said softly, and the command in his voice brought spots of hectic colour to Marina's high cheekbones.

'Can you tell me, then,' she said in a voice that shook with suppressed anger, 'what this girl was doing in your bed?'

'She was *on* it, not in it,' Anton corrected gravely. He met Alex's eyes with a lift of one eyebrow. 'As to what she was doing here, only she can say. Would you care to tell us, Alex?'

'I came here to study the paintings,' Alex repeated through gritted teeth. 'I've been checking all the paintings on this floor——'

'Rubbish!' Marina snapped.

'It's true.'

'Are you trying to deny that you were waiting for Anton on that bed?'

'I——' The force of the question struck home. She *had* been waiting for Anton. It was true. And with bitter irony, he was preparing to take another woman to that very bed! A flush rose to her face, and Marina turned with a triumphant sneer to Anton.

'Look, she admits it by her face! Anton, tell this English lover of yours to get out.'

'I'm only too pleased to be going,' Alex retorted, striding into the drawing-room with eyes full of tears.

Anton's fingers bit into her arm, stopping her dead in her tracks.

'Alex is not my lover,' he said softly. 'And *I* say who

comes and goes in this house.'

'Do you think I'm so gullible, Anton?' Marina pulled a cigarette from her crocodile-skin handbag, and lit it with a little dagger of electric flame. She exhaled a plume of blue smoke. 'What kind of woman is found lying on a man's bed?' she asked bitterly. 'I could see on her face that she was dreaming of you. Only a mistress would behave like that. A mistress or a——'

'Enough!' Anton grated, cutting short the ugly word.

'What about you?' Alex said shakily. 'Why were you in Anton's bedroom, anyway?' She jerked her arm out of Anton's fingers, and faced them both with a white, tearful face. 'There you stand, the two of you, arguing hypocritically between yourselves. But you must have come in here to——'

'Marina came here to discuss a business deal,' Anton said sharply, his face grim. 'She was going to the bathroom to wash her hands.' He pointed to a briefcase and a pile of papers at an ebony-and-hide desk in the drawing-room. 'Marina happens to have a very large interest in Telescan, Alex.' He glanced at the Princess. 'She was about to give me the details of a new share arrangement.'

For a second, Alex almost believed him. And then Marina's sneering voice broke the spell.

'You don't have to keep up pretences before this commoner, Anton,' she said, exhaling smoke like a gorgeous black dragon. She smiled pityingly at Alex. 'Come, let's all behave like adults, yes? I can understand that you found this girl desirable.'

'You can?' Anton murmured, his passionate mouth quirking into a wry line.

'Of course,' Marina shrugged. 'She is young and not unattractive. Even virginal. But now you must agree that this ridiculous *affaire* cannot continue.'

'There is no *affaire*,' Alex snapped, 'except that between you and Anton!'

'In which you have been a minor interruption,' Marina agreed coolly. She turned back to Anton. 'I can forgive you, *caro mio*. Simply tell me that it's all over, and send her back to London.' She laid a black-gloved hand caressingly on Anton's arm. 'And then you and I can continue our business. *D'accordo*?'

'You are very generous, Marina,' Anton said mildly. 'But I'm afraid Miss Lacey still has business here. And I have no intention of asking her to leave until she has finished what she came here to do.'

'Well, you can forget it,' Alex retorted, 'because I'm leaving for London tonight!'

'Very sensible,' Marina purred. 'After all, it would be very embarrassing to remain here now, wouldn't it?'

'Don't think for a minute that I'm leaving because of you,' Alex retorted, her mouth a taut line. 'You don't impress me, Princess. I'm leaving for my own reasons.'

'You're not leaving at all,' Anton corrected her quietly.

'Just try and stop me!' she challenged, her eyes blazing.

'You seem to forget that you're under contract, Miss Lacey.' His voice cut like a whip. 'If you try and leave now, I'll make damned sure that Carvel's of the Strand suffer for it!'

'That's blackmail,' Alex whispered.

Marina ground out her cigarette with a suppressed exclamation of disgust.

'Anton, for God's sake! Let's end this charade. Send your little English lover home, and promise me you'll end this romance right now.'

'How can anyone end something that doesn't exist?' he rejoined in his deep voice. 'This argument is very unseemly. I intend to stop it now.' He walked to the tray of drinks under the big landscape, and poured whisky into three crystal tumblers as the women watched in silence. His magnificent face was calm as he returned with the glasses, giving them one each.

'Now. Miss Lacey is going nowhere, and nor are you. There are no plots, no affairs, no secrets. And if there are any ultimatums to be delivered, I will deliver them.'

'Anton——' Marina began, but he cut her short.

'Enough. We'll have no more of this argument. Your very good health, ladies.'

He drank. Alex stood silent and trembling for a minute.

'I'm afraid you can't solve this problem quite so easily, Anton. I'm going home tonight, whether you like it or not. And Carvel's can send someone else to do this job. If they choose to sack me, that's just too bad.'

'Alex,' he said gently, 'don't provoke me. You'll regret it.'

'You couldn't hurt me any more now if you burned me alive,' she said in a low, quivering voice. 'And I don't want this drink, thanks.'

She walked over to the little table, and put the heavy tumbler down on the silver tray.

'You see?' Marina's voice came from behind her. 'At least the child has a sense of shame. Let her go, Anton. Don't cling to this whim of yours——'

'Marina, hold your tongue,' he said sharply. 'Alex, what's the matter?'

She was staring with wide eyes at the huge landscape in front of her. Slowly she reached out to touch it with slender fingers.

'Was this painting in this room when you inherited Castelnero?' she asked, turning to face him.

'Yes,' he nodded. 'I don't especially like it. I've been meaning to move it for some time.'

'Come, come,' Marina scorned. 'No more tricks——'

'Why are you so interested?' Anton asked. 'It's a very dull piece of work. Only the sky is good.'

'Yes,' she nodded, 'the sky is very good.'

The painting was a dark landscape in nineteeth-century taste. In the foreground, a river wound through heavy undergrowth, painted with almost crude thickness. A sombre forest spread up the far bank, the tall trees silhouetted against the evening sky. Suddenly, all the misery and horror of the argument she had just lived through began to fade.

'Anton!' she called, 'come and look!'

He was beside her in an instant, his beautiful grey eyes enquiring on her face.

'What's so special?'

'Look there—through that tree-top.'

He followed her finger.

'Yes,' he nodded. 'There's some sort of building there, behind the trees. I've always thought it was a church.'

'Oh, please!' Marina's laugh was brittle. 'These games are for children, Anton. Are you going to let this little creature weave her spell over you again?'

'It's a church,' Alex agreed. Excitement was bubbling up inside her. 'But it doesn't look as though it was painted by the same artist who did the trees, does it?'

'No,' he agreed, studying it more closely. 'I've noticed that. It looks older, better painted. So is the sky.'

'Yes,' she agreed excitedly, studying the wide expanse of pale blue, cloud-flecked sky. 'My God, I wonder if it can be——?'

'Your amateur dramatics are very interesting, Miss Lacey,' Marina Bergatrice said contemptuously, walking up to join them. 'But you were just leaving.'

'I think it's a palimpsest,' Alex told Anton with sparkling violet eyes. 'I'm sure of it, in fact.'

'A palimpsest?' Marina narrowed her almond eyes. 'What are you babbling about? What's a palimpsest?'

'It's a painting that's been executed on top of an earlier work,' Anton murmured. 'Am I right?'

'Exactly,' Alex nodded. 'Oh, Anton, do you realise what this could mean?'

'No,' he smiled, draining his whisky. 'What could it mean?'

'This could be one of the most exciting finds in the art world for twenty years!'

'What nonsense,' Marina scoffed. 'Anton, we've got business to discuss.'

Alex stepped back to study the painting from a distance. Her heart was thudding with excitement and joy. Anton watched her face, a slight smile still on his lips.

'Well?' he prompted. 'Let us into the secret, my dear Alex.'

She looked at him, then struck her forehead.

'I never told you! In all the excitement of the past few days, I clean forgot to tell you!'

'Well, now's your chance.' Taking her arm, he ushered her to an armchair. 'But let's all sit down like civilised people. Come, Marina.'

Her eyes dark and suspicious, Marina settled her elegant body on a sofa in front of Alex, wrapping the black splendour of her sable coat around herself.

Anton sat down, crossing his legs and leaning back.

'Now,' he said. 'What did you forget to tell me about?'

'About the Canaletto!'

'What Canaletto?' Marina asked silkily.

'The one in this house. Wilbert Carvel did some research about Castelnero before I came here—and he discovered that someone in this house once bought a large painting of Venice that might be—that almost certainly *was*—a Canaletto. That's why he sent me here—because I know a little about Canaletto's style. I cleaned three big landscapes for the National Gallery earlier this year. I was actually due to take three weeks' leave in the South of France, but Mr Carvel persuaded me to to take this job on instead.'

'How very fortunate,' Anton murmured, his smoky eyes surveying her thoughtfully.

'The Canaletto may still be in this house!' she said excitedly. 'And I think it may be that painting over there!'

'*That?*' Marina Bergatrice's voice was heavy with derision. 'That's no Canaletto, you little goose!'

'It may be,' she replied, 'under all that mucky river and forest. Those trees may be painted over one of the greatest achievements of eighteenth-century Venice!'

'Pah! Who would paint over a Canaletto?' Marina asked scornfully.

Anton's eyes were bright.

'Stranger things have happened,' he said thoughtfully. 'Nineteenth-century painters tended to be very contemptuous about the work of the century before them. There are countless examples of great eighteenth-century canvases being "improved" or painted over by Victorian artists.'

'That's right,' Alex agreed eagerly, staring from Anton to the big landscape on the wall in front of them.

'But—a Canaletto!' Marina exclaimed. 'Who would do such a thing? It would be worth hundreds of thousands!'

'Even Canaletto was despised by the Victorians,' Alex said. 'One of the best, which I did some work on last year, was actually cut into pieces by some nineteenth-century owner to fit a spare frame he had!' She gazed at the painting, drinking it in with bright eyes. 'That sky! I know his style so well. I'm sure it's a Canaletto!'

'But what about the trees and river?' Anton queried. 'Could you get them off without damaging the painting underneath?'

'It would take weeks,' she mused, her mind

whirling. 'Maybe with an initial bath in turps to soften the top layer——'

'But it could be done?'

'Yes,' she said firmly. 'It could be done. But this is a job for someone with years of experience.'

'Aren't you capable of it?' he asked.

'Of course she isn't,' Marina interrupted sharply. 'She's only a child.'

'I'm afraid the Princess is right,' Alex gritted. 'I wouldn't dare take something like this on. The authority in this field is a man called Oberholzer, in Vienna. He'd be your best bet.'

'What a shame,' Anton purred, stretching like a leopard. 'Now we'll never know.'

'What?' Alex blinked.

'I said, now we'll never know.'

'But Karl Oberholzer would clean it for you,' Alex protested in surprise. 'This is a tremendously important find, Anton——'

'Too important to trust to Oberholzer,' Anton nodded. 'I want you to do this job, Alex.'

'Don't be a fool, Anton,' Marina snarled.

'But, Anton,' Alex protested, 'I'm only twenty——'

'Your eyes are the sharper and your hands the steadier,' he rejoined calmly. 'Karl Oberholzer is an alcoholic, Alex. Everybody knows that.'

'He may be an alcoholic, but he's the best in the world——'

'He *was* the best in the world,' Anton corrected her gently. 'You must have heard what he did to that Botticelli.'

'Mistakes happen,' she replied. 'He used the wrong solvent, and took off more paint then he intended——'

'And destroyed a priceless work of art. Besides costing his client practically a million pounds. Oberholzer's had his day, Alex. His mind is wandering now. He's done his best work, and I shouldn't be surprised if he's already retired. It's time for someone else to take his place.'

'There are dozens of others ready to do just that,' she sighed.

'And none of them are any more talented or qualified than you.'

'Anton, how can you think of it?' Marina hissed.

'I trust Alex,' he said simply.

'But I haven't ever done anything on this scale before!'

'You've worked on Canalettos before. If the National Gallery trusts you, Alexandra Lacey, then I'm prepared to trust you.'

'But——'

'Oh, come on! You know you can do it. Well, don't you?'

She sat, frozen, and then nodded slowly.

'Yes,' she said quietly, 'I know I can do it.'

'You're mad, child——'

'She's not mad,' Anton contradicted. He rose, and went to study the huge canvas. 'Yes,' he said thoughtfully, 'it *is* a palimpsest. And that sky could easily be Canaletto. Trouble is, the whole thing's so damned dark——' He turned to face Alex, who was watching with parted lips, her auburn hair framing her oval face. 'Will you do it? Because if you won't, I swear nobody else will.'

'Yes,' she said slowly, 'I'll do it.' It was sinking in now that he was right. She *was* capable of an immense challenge like this. Maybe she wouldn't have been ready six months ago. Maybe not even a week ago. Maybe her readiness had came through the maturity that Anton de Cassis had brought to her emotions.

But for whatever reason, she knew that she was ready now. And without vanity or fear, she knew that if anyone could bring the painting hidden by that crude forest back to the light of day, then she could.

'If you want me to,' she said again, 'I'll do it.'

Marina sat silent and deadly as a cobra, her face white with barely-controlled anger.

Anton nodded, as though expecting her reply.

'Good. Then I trust this means the end of your precipitate plans to leave tonight?'

'Yes,' she agreed softly. 'I'm staying.'

His eyes held hers, their power sending that old, sweet thrill through her veins.

'Well,' he purred, 'let's all drink to a successful undertaking!'

Marina Bergatrice watched him drink with dark, almond eyes.

'We shall see,' she said slowly. 'We shall see.'

Two days' work confirmed Alex's suspicions beyond the shadow of a doubt. Through the patch of heavily-painted foliage she had chosen to start on, the outline of a gondola on a canal could be seen.

Unmistakably Canaletto.

'The principle of the whole thing,' she told a wildly elated Wilbert Carvel down the telephone, 'is that the later paint hasn't set as hard as the earlier paint. It's just that fraction more soluble—so with careful use of solvents, I can clean off the surface layers without touching the stuff underneath.'

'For God's sake don't miscalculate that fraction,' Wilbert pleaded. 'This is the major art event of the year! There's a lot of discreet excitement in top circles here—and I've just released a statement to *The Times*. This is going to put Carvel's at the top of the league, Alex. Bless you and your sharp eyes!'

'I haven't finished the job yet,' she smiled. 'I could easily fail. Or worse still, ruin the whole thing.'

'You won't,' Wilbert yelped. 'Will you? Listen, have you sounded Anton de Cassis out about selling it yet?'

'No,' she replied, biting her lip. 'Somehow I don't think he will want to sell it, Wilbert. He's not exactly short of cash.'

'Never mind, the publicity is fantastic anyway. Bless you again, Alex—you're a genius. Aren't you glad I persuaded you to take this job on now?'

'Yes and no,' she said wryly. 'Yes and no, Wilbert.'

The Canaletto absorbed her. It provided a perfect kind of therapy for her. Therapy in that as she wiped patiently, skilfully at the old canvas, she could let her mind run free, let it explore her feelings for Anton de Cassis. So much was yet unresolved. So much was uncertain.

So much was yet to come. She was able to bury herself in her work, to hide away from him; and he, with an unerring instinct, let her alone, as though sensing that she needed solitude and peace in which to settle her turbulent emotions.

If this was love, she thought with a wry smile, then there was one important thing about it that the songs and poems never mentioned.

It hurt.

And Anton fascinated her more than ever. As they ate together in the evenings, usually with a rose-candle burning between them, she could scarcely take her eyes off him. He was so wonderful, so virile; everything about him intrigued her, the golden velevet of his skin, the contours of his face, the strength in his hands, the passionate lines of that bewitching mouth. He would look up and catch her eyes on him, making her duck her head and pick at her bread like a schoolgirl on her first date, her heart thudding. Then she would mutter an excuse, and run off as soon as possible to the huge canvas she had stretched out in the upstairs studio.

Marina hadn't made an appearance. Alex had the uneasy feeling that she was brewing something unpleasant in the interim. But Kitty Kowalski had paid a visit to Castelnero, and had padded through the great house in her sneakers, alternately overawed at its grandeur and Alex's good fortune, and irreverently amused at her friend's apparent calm.

'You act as though this sort of thing happened to you every day,' she teased. 'Doesn't *anything* excite you?'

'If only you knew,' Alex said ruefully, dabbing at the canvas with a swab.

Kitty watched her slender, skilled fingers with sympathetic eyes.

'Got it bad, huh?'

'Bad,' Alex confirmed. 'Or very, very good. I can't tell which.'

'Uh-huh. And he hasn't tried any hanky-panky with you yet?'

'Well——' Alex paused, confused. Kitty's frankness was sometimes a shock to her British reticence. 'Actually——'

'He has, but you've put out the red light?'

'Something like that.'

'I think I get it,' said Kitty. 'It's a big thing to some girls.'

'What is?' Alex looked up from her work with puzzled violet eyes.

'This virtue thing. Speaking for myself, I couldn't wait to get rid of mine. Lost it years ago.'

'Oh,' said Alex, nonplussed. Then, realising what Kitty meant, she set to work again, flushing slightly. 'I see. Does it show that much?'

'What—that you're a maiden pure? Sure.' Kitty grinned. 'Written all over your gorgeous face.'

'Oh dear!'

'There's nothing to "oh dear" about.' Kitty cocked her head to study Alex quizzically. 'Frankly, I really envy you, Alex.'

'You do?'

'Yes. Some day, when I fall in love with Mr Right, and marry him, I'm really going to wish I could—well, come to him the virgin bride. I know it sounds horribly corny, but there it is. Pity. Still——' she brightened, '—maybe I can fake it!'

'He won't love you a scrap the less for it,' said Alex, laughing at Kitty's wicked grin.

'Sure. But I guess I'm a real dyed-in-the-wool romantic at heart.'

'There's nothing romantic about dying of thirst with the water at the end of the corridor,' Alex said drily.

Kitty laughed, then shook her head compassionately. 'You really do have it bad! What does he feel about you?'

'I think he's going to marry Marina Bergatrice, if that's what you mean,' Alex replied. Her mouth tightened, and she studied the area she had just cleaned with deep, hyacinth eyes. 'I don't know what he feels, Kitty. I know he wants me physically. I don't think it's anything more than that.' She sighed. 'And he's having an affair with Marina right now.'

'Are you sure?'

'Just about.'

'Listen, Alex, only a real cad would proposition one female while he's still got the other one's kisses hot on his lips, so to speak. And Anton de Cassis doesn't strike me as your genuine cad. Haven't you made some mistake?'

'Maybe.' Alex wiped at the canvas, and peered closer. 'There it is.'

'What?'

'St Mark's. See that golden cross? That'll be the top of St Mark's Cathedral.' She tapped the centre of the canvas, still covered in the hideous river and trees. 'It'll be under there, taking up the centre of the painting.'

'Clever girl! Whadd'ya know?'

And that evening Alex uncovered the whole top section of the cathedral. The composition was beginning to become apparent now. It was a characteristically vast, breathtaking panorama, the sort of huge vista that Canaletto revelled in.

In the foreground was the Bay of St Mark, its blue waters thronged with gondolas and barges. Straight ahead was the Cathedral, its massive shape dominating the centre of the painting. To the left, the great square, no doubt filled with people, maybe even a procession. And all around, the buildings of Venice, humble and grandiose, painted with the love that only a Venetian could bring to his subject.

She had worked with meticulous skill, and so far—touch wood—not the slightest trace of damage to the original paint was apparent. The colours were coming up as fresh and vivid as though they had been painted yesterday. Maybe the coating of Victorian paint had even acted as a protecting film over the precious original.

She had rigged up two bright spotlights to work by, and as the summer night stole over Venice, she stayed at her bench, working constantly at the painting, her mind wandering over the events of the past weeks, trying to assimilate it all.

At around ten o'clock, the door opened softly, bringing with it the aroma of freshly-made coffee and the clink of a tray.

'Thank you, Umberto,' Alex called without turning round. 'Just put the tray down.'

She bent tiredly over her work, an ache of tension beginning to spread across her shoulders and neck. She had been working so very hard. Maybe it was time to take a break.

She twisted her neck, trying to ease away the strain—then started as a pair of strong, gentle hands slid across the aching muscle. She didn't have to ask who it was.

He dug his thumbs gently into the flesh of her shoulders, rubbing away the kinks and knots with expert care. For a second she sat rigid, then slowly let her head droop forward so that her shining hair cascaded down on to her breast.

His hands were wonderful, massaging a delicious warmth into her tired muscles, spreading a languorous delight through her whole body.

'I couldn't stay away any longer,' he growled. 'And it's high time you packed it in. You're exhausted.'

'Oh, that's so good,' she sighed as his fingers kneaded her delicate deltoid muscles, his thumbs caressing the satiny skin at the back of her neck.

'You've done so much, Alex. And so very well. I knew I was right to insist you did this job.' He lifted her drooping head to massage under her jawline with gentle, knowing fingers. 'But I didn't intend you to work yourself to death.'

'Hmm,' she groaned, blissfully letting her head roll back against the sure strength of his arms. 'Where did you learn to do this?'

'I had a Japanese friend,' he replied. 'She taught me lots of things.'

'She?' Alex didn't disguise the disapproval in her voice.

'Little Puritan,' he smiled. 'You must admit that I'm good.'

'You're very good.'

'You're very tense. At least, you were.' He kissed the top of her head, his hands running gently across the top of her shoulders. 'Feeling better now?'

'Very relaxed,' she smiled. 'What did you mean, you couldn't stay away?'

'You know exactly what I mean,' he said, his voice deep. 'I've been sitting in my study, thinking of you sitting up here——'

'—thinking of you sitting down in your study,' she finished. Damn! She was so languorously relaxed now that her tongue was running away with her again.

'I've brought you some coffee.' His hands were warm on her shoulders.

'Coffee's not what I want,' she whispered.

'Alex . . .'

His hands slid caressingly down her chest and under her cotton shirt, cupping her breasts. A shudder of passion made her arch her back, her eyes closing of their own accord. Her own hands rose slowly to rest on his, pressing them lightly against her tautening flesh.

'That's not relaxing at all,' she said huskily, her heart thudding in her throat.

'It's not meant to be.'

She could hear the desire thick in his voice, and it sent a slow thrill of delight down into her loins. Dear heaven, she wanted to sob, can't you see how much I love you? Don't you know what you do to me?

'I want you, Alex,' Anton whispered, his breath warm in her silky hair. The peaks of her breasts had hardened to thrust against his palms, and she pressed his hands convulsively against her body before pulling them away, and spinning round in her chair to face him.

'For God's sake,' she cried shakily, 'don't do this to me!'

He stared down at the tears in her wide eyes, his mouth slanting into a wry smile.

'Why do we do this to each other?' he asked. Taking her oval face in his hands, he kissed the tears from her lids with warm lips; then, taking her by the hands, raised her, and led her over to the sofa against the far wall.

'Drink your coffee,' he commanded. As she sipped the fragrant, scalding brew, he continued, 'I'm sorry, Alex. I don't want to torment either of us. You know how I feel about you.'

'I'm sorry, too. I guess I'm overtired.'

'Sure you are.' He watched her face as she drank, his eyes fathomless. 'You're so lovely, my dear one. Your skin feels like hot satin under my hands, and your hair smells of summer. Don't blame me for wanting to touch you.'

Don't you think I want to touch you? her mind asked him fiercely. Aloud, she said, 'I don't blame you for anything, Anton.'

'Is that coffee doing you good?'

'Yes, it's lovely. Have you had a good day?'

'Indifferent,' he shrugged, and pulled up a chair to prop his feet up on, leaning back with a sigh.

'For a successful businessman, you sound rather jaded,' she smiled.

'Business isn't always pleasure,' he grimaced. 'Sometimes it's nothing but a damned worry.' She waited, hoping he was going to confide in her further, but he smiled tiredly. 'Sorry—you don't want to hear my troubles. You're working wonders with that Canaletto.' He took one of her hands in his own, and studied it with hooded eyes. 'Clever hands. Beautiful hands.' He lifted her palm to his lips, and kissed it gently. The gesture touched her deeply—it was so tender, so unexpected. He slipped his fingers through hers, and laid the back of her hand against his cheek, leaning against her slightly as he closed his eyes.

She could feel the roughness of his day-old beard, and as she watched him, devouring every line of his face with intent eyes, it dawned on her with a pang that he was looking unusually care-worn.

Aching to comfort him, she asked, 'Is everything all right, Anton?'

'Everything's fine,' he said without opening his eyes. A slight smile stirred on his lips. 'Everything's fine now. You're so good to be with, Alex.'

'Am I?' she asked. God, she so needed to be told!

'You're the only person I've ever known who can make me unwind like this,' he said, his voice soft with relaxation. 'When I come to you, it's like sitting beside a slow, deep river. You bring me peace, Alex . . .' His eyes opened lazily, and he rolled his head to look at her. There was a glint in his eyes as he added, 'On the other hand, there are times when you're about the most unrestful woman I've come across.' Their eyes locked, and she knew he could sense the longing in her, the quickening desire for his lips on hers, his arms around her. His fingers tightened around her own, hard and masterful.

'No,' he commanded, 'don't look at me like that, damn it! You make me burn.' She tore her eyes away from the answering desire in those smoky depths, feeling her face grow hot.

'Sorry,' she muttered.

'You don't really trust me, do you?' he asked gently.

'Why do you say that?' she blinked.

'I can sense it. Not now. But sometimes, in your eyes—do you think I'm going to hurt you?'

'Not deliberately,' she said slowly. 'I just——'

'What?' he prompted, his fingers tight around hers.

'Well,' she said, meeting his eyes, 'sometimes I think you're unaware of the effect you have on other people. You don't know quite how much other people feel for you.' She dropped her eyes. 'I don't think you'd ever harm me by intent. But you might do so without meaning to.'

'Do you really think me so insensitive?' Anton asked softly.

She shook her head mutely. If only he knew how deeply she wanted to believe in him, how much she needed to know that he was aware of her growing love for him, that he felt at least a part of what she felt.

'We're so different,' she said uncertainly.

'Do you really think so?' He sat up, turning to face her, and slid her hand around his neck, so that she was forced to half-embrace him with an appearance of confidence about his body that she was very far from feeling. His eyes were serious. 'We're not different, Alex. We're both loners, both achievers. We've chosen different careers, different countries. But inwardly we're the same. Don't you feel it?'

'But you're so outward-going, so brave! I prefer to stand back, keep out of the way if I can——'

'You can't keep out of the way this time,' he said urgently. 'Didn't we both lose our parents young? And haven't we both had to make our way in the world alone? Don't you sense that in our hearts we understand one another? We're not identical, Alex—thank God for that. Yet I've never known two people so compatible as you and I are. You give me peace—and yet you thrill me to the core. You make me laugh—and yet you tug at my heart. And if you deny that,' he said, touching her lips with a warning forefinger, 'you're a liar, Alex Lacey.'

What he had said was flowing through her soul like strong wine, making her want to throw herself into his arms, telling him that it was true, that they were so perfectly matched it made her ache——

Instead, she dropped her head, letting her thick hair fall in a dark curtain on to her lap.

'There are hundreds of women in this city alone who could make you feel the same,' she sighed. 'Marina Bergatrice, for example.'

'Oh, Marina,' he groaned. 'God, I'm getting sick of hearing her name . . .'

In the pause that followed, a distant clock somewhere in the house chimed midnight. Anton drew her forward, and kissed her lightly on the lips.

'It's late,' he smiled. 'And we must to bed. Not, alas, to the same bed,' he growled, his eyes passionate on her mouth. He kissed her again, this time leaving a little dagger of flame burning in her heart. 'But I'm confident you'll think of me before you go to sleep,' he grinned wickedly. 'Come on, Alex. It's time all the toys were put back in their boxes!'

CHAPTER SEVEN

ALEX came down from her studio one afternoon, two days later, in the hopes of finding coffee and biscuits in the beautiful drawing-room. Anton's voice from the hall telephone told her that he had come home early. Waving to him across the hall, she followed the aroma of freshly-percolated coffee into the rose-coloured drawing-room.

An unexpected sight awaited her there. Lying on the red and green Kashkai rug was something that might have dropped from outer space. It was a gleaming cylinder of some kind of steel alloy, its complicated surface etched with exquisitely-detailed circuitry. Three antennae had been positioned at one end, while at the other there was a complicated mesh bowl, like a radar screen.

The space-age technology was incongruous in this classical eighteenth-century room. She squatted to study it more closely. The Telescan logo was emblazoned on the satin-smooth surface.

So this was an example of Anton's craft? Marvelling at the incredible detail and precision of the instrument, Alex touched the cold metal almost reverently.

'Like it?'

She turned to look at Anton, who had come into the room, and was pouring coffee.

'It's beautiful,' she smiled. 'But that's merely an aesthetic judgment. It'd be a wow on a modern sculpture exhibition. What is it?'

'E367,' he said, and there was a sparkle of pride in the grey eyes. 'The first of the new generation of satellite relays.'

'You mean—this thing goes up into outer space?' she blinked, accepting the cup of coffee he gave her.

'Sure.' He kissed her on the lips. 'How's Signor Canaletto?'

'Fine. But this——' She gestured at the satellite. 'Why, it's no bigger than a hi-fi set!'

'That's the beauty of it,' he grinned. 'You don't need a huge rocket to get these into orbit. And they don't fall back to earth, giving everybody heart failure in the process.' He stooped. 'Look,' he commanded, sliding a little hatch open. The interior was a solid mass of coloured wiring and miniaturised electronic gear. 'She can relay television programmes right round the world. Or carry S.O.S. messages from the tiniest transmitter. Or maybe, one day, talk to people from another star.'

Alex stared at the thing with new awe.

'Your design?' she hazarded.

'From top to tail. I practically built the thing with my own hands.' His eyes were bright. 'It's not exactly profitable, building these things—but it makes a welcome change from closed-circuit television systems. And it takes Telescan's reputation sky-high, if you'll forgive the pun.'

'It's beautiful,' she said again, touching the satellite hesitantly. 'I just can't imagine designing and building something like this . . .'

'It's only a minor miracle of science,' he smiled gently. 'Don't let the complexity of the thing dazzle you. It's just a flying television tower.'

'A tower that goes into outer space,' she corrected quietly. 'A tower that can speak to the stars. I think it's wonderful, Anton.'

'Flattery will get you everywhere,' he assured her. 'Would you like to know how it works?'

'Yes,' she nodded firmly. 'I want to know everything about it.'

He lost her within thirty seconds, but she kept

nodding solemnly, watching his face. The face of a technician who loved his work, who knew he was superbly skilled. Somehow, watching Anton with his satellite made her love him all the more. The almost miraculous technology was a key to the other side of his nature, the brilliance of his mind. A piercing intelligence which she knew he played down, as though he instinctively felt that people wouldn't be comfortable with it, would be intimidated by it.

But the man who could design a thing like this was little short of brilliant. Not just inspired genius, but the brilliance that meant hours and months of careful, unflinching work, hours of calculations and experiments, hours of testing and re-testing. Loneliness, self-discipline, a power of concentration which would be impossible in someone of less character than Anton de Cassis.

No wonder he had chosen not to use the title Prince! That was a title from the past, a meaningless piece of snobbery. A designer like this, capable of thrusting his mind to the limits of space, capable of throwing his imagination beyond the bounds of this world he lived in, needed no false titles. She had often thought of Anton as a Renaissance lord. Now she saw him as a man of the future.

Without thinking, her hand reached out to brush his cheek tenderly. Surprised, he looked up from the bank of circuits.

'Am I losing you?' he asked.

'You lost me ten minutes ago,' she said softly. 'But don't stop. I love to hear your voice.'

'Sorry,' he smiled. 'I tend to forget that this is all a mystery to most people.'

'It's a very wonderful mystery,' she said, shaking her head slowly. 'I spend my time scraping carefully at the past—and you reach into the future.'

'Your work is no less important than mine,' he said gently. 'If we lost the past, the future wouldn't be worth reaching for.' He kicked the satellite softly with an inward smile. 'I've brought my baby home for some last-minute checks. Later this afternoon, she's going off to Milan. From there, in three weeks' time, she goes to America to be launched, along with a lot of other scientific and technological gadgetry.'

'You lead an exciting life,' she smiled. But there was real respect behind the teasing.

'E367 isn't a very glamorous name,' he mused. 'I was thinking of calling her something more personal. Say, Alexandra 1.'

'You're teasing me,' she said uncertainly.

'Not at all,' he assured her. 'Naming is a very important business. And Alexandra is a very beautiful name. As you are a very beautiful woman.' He tapped her nose. 'Don't look so stunned. Have I your permission to call it Alexandra?'

'Of course,' she said, breathless.

'Alexandra 1 it is then,' he said with a quiet smile. 'Next year there'll be an Alexandra 2 and 3. How does it feel to know your name will be going half-way to the stars?'

'I—I don't know what to say,' she stammered, putting her hand to her hot face. 'It's a great honour——'

'Don't take it so seriously,' he chided her. 'Ninety-nine per cent of the world's population won't even know it's up there. And the other one per cent won't care.' He slid an arm around her waist, and walked her to the window. 'But we'll know,' he smiled.

'And we'll care,' she finished for him. She was feeling distinctly weak in the legs. 'Anton, I'm still at a loss. What have I done to deserve an honour like this?'

'I'll tell you,' he said, staring out at the canal with serious eyes. 'You found that Canaletto, Alex.'

'But that's a relatively minor thing compared to——'

'It's not minor at all,' he said gravely. 'You can't possibly know how important that Canaletto is to me. I don't want to bore you with technical details, Alex— but your turning up that painting has been the best thing that's ever happened to me.'

'But how——?'

'In fact, if it wasn't for that painting up there, Alexandra I might never make it half-way to the stars. Now,' he finished, turning to face her, 'let's not talk about this any more. One day I'll tell you what I mean, and what you've done for me. Right now, I've got my mind on a little break for us tomorrow.'

'What sort of break?' she wanted to know.

'A day in the sun. There are some beautiful islands near here, mostly quite uninhabited. I thought we'd pack a picnic lunch, a bottle of champagne, maybe an umbrella—and take the launch out to the furthest and loveliest of the islands. And just lie in the sun. Or swim. Or collect shells. And forget all our worries and responsibilities. What do you say?'

'It sounds like Paradise,' she sighed.

'It will be. If I can keep my hands off you,' he smiled.

'I'll wear my overalls,' she grinned back.

'Then you'll come?'

Alex drained her cup with an ironic tilt to her eyebrows.

'You didn't really think I was going to refuse, did you?'

'I would have simply kidnapped you if you had,' he answered. His eyes sparkled. 'But I'm glad I didn't have to!' He stooped to pick up the satellite. 'Right now I have to make some minor adjustments to your namesake.' He surveyed her wickedly over the gleaming surface. 'And frankly, I wish you were as easy to understand as your namesake is!'

The sea was warm and gentle, and so limpid that Alex

could see the pebbles and sand at the bottom, in the turquoise depths beneath her own legs.

She rolled on to her back and floated on the lapping waves, staring through half-closed lashes at the exquisite duck's-egg blue of a Mediterranean sky. Anton had been right; this was Paradise.

The sun was deliciously hot. It had already warmed the surface layer of the water, and there was hardly a breath of wind to disturb the utter peace of the morning.

Bresolo was the farthest out of the Venetian islands, so far from the city that they might have been marooned in the Pacific. In fact, Bresolo looked more like a desert island than anything Alex had ever seen. Little more than a long sandbank extending for a few hundred yards, it was covered in rustling palms and clumps of long, waving grass. The sand was white and beautifully clean, and were it not for the majestic shape of Venice, rising out of the sea a few miles to the west, Bresolo might have been a Pacific atoll, two thousand miles from the nearest continent.

From the beach, the sounds of Anton unloading the launch drifted to her. They had set out in the cool blue of the early morning, before Venice was properly awake, and had beached the launch in the clean sand, hauling it up out of the tide's way. But as soon as the sun was hot, Alex hadn't been able to resist the sparkling water. She had stripped down to her pale blue Lycra bikini, and had plunged into the sea.

Glancing lazily at the shore, she now saw that Anton had planted the striped umbrella in the sand, and was pulling off his Sea Island Cotton shirt. She rolled on to her stomach, and broke into a smooth, efficient crawl, revelling in the stretch and play of stiff muscles. It was ages since she had swum, and she had missed it badly.

When at last she stopped, panting, to tread water, Anton was beside her, his dark hair sleeked back.

'I had no idea you were such a water baby,' he grinned. 'I had trouble keeping up with you.'

'I was school champion,' she told him proudly. 'Though that seems a long time ago now. Ouch, I'm stiff!'

'I know practically nothing about you, Alex,' he said, reaching out to brush a wet tendril of her hair away from her cheek. 'Caught your breath yet? I'll race you to that rock, and then I want to hear all about how you were school champion. Right?'

He set off fast, his brown shoulders cleaving the water in a foam of white, and she followed in pursuit. It was heaven to really extend her body again. The three years at Carvel's had been short of exercise, and the past few days hunched over the Canaletto had left her feeling confined. As she waded ashore with Anton, her chest was heaving with exertion.

'Boy,' she spluttered, hauling her wet hair back to cascade over her shoulders, 'you're not a bad swimmer yourself! Gosh, that feels good . . .'

She collapsed on to her towel, luxuriating in the warmth of the sand beneath. Anton stood, hands on hips, smiling down at her.

'Is it too early for champagne?'

'At ten o'clock in the morning?' she queried with a giggle. 'Of course not!'

'My opinion exactly.' He walked back to the waterline to retrieve the bottle he had thrust into the wet sand to cool. Alex lay on one elbow, watching him.

He was magnificently built, his skin tanned a deep honey-gold, and he moved with all the lithe grace of some great hunting cat. Fascinated, she watched the planes of muscle shifting in his back as he walked. His shoulders were broad, and packed with hard power; but his torso tapered down to the supple waist that was taut with flat muscles.

He grinned at her as he brought the bottle back, as

stunningly handsome as some sea-god emerging from
the waves. The black costume he wore was narrow
enough to make her heart thud uncomfortably, and the
dark triangle of hair across his hard chest extended in
a narrow band down his stomach and abdomen, a
reminder of the potent sexuality alive in this man.

'What are you staring at?' he asked as he knelt down
next to her, ripping off the foil on the neck of the
bottle.

'I was trying to read the label,' she lied in confusion.

'It's a Moët & Chandon Epernay,' he told her. 'I
hope it's cold enough.'

'I'm not fussy,' she smiled. Through lowered lashes,
she watched the intricate play of the muscles in his
forearms as he twisted the cork out. The way he was
kneeling had brought the long muscles of his thighs
into relief. Suddenly she was looking forward to the
champagne; her throat had gone as dry as a bone.

She would be lucky to get through this day
unscathed. Anton de Cassis was a formidably
attractive man fully clothed. Almost naked, as he was
now, he was devastating—the archetypal man, virile
and magnificent.

The cork exploded out of the bottle with a gush of
champagne, and she held her glass out to be filled.

'To you,' he smiled, his eyes meeting hers.

'And to you.'

The champagne was dry, cool, and delicious. It
carried the fragrance of another summer's grapes,
sparkling with a tiny, fine bead of bubbles.

Selfconsciously, Alex tugged her top carefully over
her breasts, wishing the material weren't quite so thin,
and rolled on one hip to straighten the narrow bottom.
He watched her with an ironic smile.

'You're on holiday, Alex. And I'm not about to eat
you!'

He drank, his grey eyes drifting over her body, from
her face down to her flat stomach and neat navel,

down to the tantalising triangle of blue Lycra that was all the bottom of her costume consisted of. A quiver went through her, as though his gaze had been an actual, erotic caress, and blushing hotly, she rolled on to her stomach.

His chuckle was amused, sexy.

'I guess you are safer that way,' he murmured. 'Though why you should be ashamed of your body defeats me. It's beautiful. And also strong. That's unusual for a woman. Did the swimming do that?'

'I suppose so,' she nodded, toying absently with her champagne glass. 'Seven years of swimming and ten of ballet.'

'I might have guessed. You've got a dancer's legs. When did you stop?'

'When I was sixteen.'

'Why?'

'Partly because it was interfering with my school-work. But the real reason was this.' She sat up, and showed him the faint white scar that ran from just above her left knee to half-way up her thigh.

'Tendon?' he asked gently, and she nodded.

'I was walking again in three weeks. But they said I'd never dance again.' Even now, the bitterness came through in her voice.

'You were good, weren't you?' he asked.

'I had some talent,' she told him with a wry smile. 'I might even have made a career as a second-string dancer. If it hadn't been for this.'

'Instead, you've made a career as a first-rate art restorer,' he said. 'And if you'd been a dancer, you might never have come to Venice.'

He leaned forward and kissed the faint scar with warm lips. The contact raised her skin in goose-flesh, making her ache to run her fingers through his thick, wet hair.

He refilled her glass, and she rolled back on to her stomach, letting the sun beat down on her back.

'Funny,' she murmured. 'When it happened, I thought my whole world had ended. Less than two years later, I thought there could be nothing better than to be a really good restorer.' She drank the delicious wine thoughtfully. 'Not having any parents, I guess I took things more seriously than other kids. I always knew that I was on my own, that I was going to have to look after myself—even while Granddad was alive. For the last five years, it was a moot point whether he was taking care of me or I was taking care of him.'

'Did you love him?'

'Very much,' she smiled. 'He was a wonderful old man, a real gentleman of the old school. Oddly enough——' she paused uncomfortably. 'Well, you remind me of him.'

'Thank you,' Anton chuckled. 'I'm only thirty-six.'

'I don't mean physically. You've just got the same perfect manners, the same sort of unruffled poise——'

'It must be the Army training,' he smiled. He reached out, and plopped a straw hat on to her head. If we're going to drink champagne in the sun, you'd better wear that. And you're going to burn without sun-tan lotion.'

Alex subsided, laying her head blissfully on her folded arms, as he undid the strap of her bikini top, and poured a little golden puddle of Ambre Solaire on to her fine skin.

'Don't stop talking, Alex. Tell me about your childhood.'

'Well—I don't remember my parents at all. They died when I was two. My only close relation was Granddad, and he brought me up.'

His fingers were smoothing the oil over her back, moulding her shoulderblades with deep, gentle strokes. It was ecstasy, sensuous and relaxing. She sighed softly as his palms slid along the springy muscles from the small of her back right up to her shoulders.

'Don't stop,' he prompted.

'Do you do this for Marina Bergatrice?' she asked lazily. Her punishment was a dig of his thumbs into her trapezoid muscles.

'Forget Marina Bergatrice,' he growled.

'But have you brought her here?' she persisted. 'Your princess?'

'No. This is Anton's island. I've only ever come here alone before. Satisfied?'

Somehow, she believed him—and was deeply glad.

'She wouldn't like it here anyway,' she said blandly. 'The sand would only get in her crown jewels.'

'Now there's a funny thing,' Anton grinned. 'I never suspected you of having such a sharp tongue, Alexandra Lacey.'

'Marina Bergatrice isn't exactly my favourite person,' she rejoined.

His strong hands pushed the tension out of her muscles, reproving her.

'Forget Marina. Tell me about Alex.'

'Are you really interested? Your life is so much more glamorous than mine.'

'I'm really interested.'

'In what, for instance?'

'Well,' he said obliquely, 'you don't wear a scrap of jewellery. That's unusual in a woman of your age.'

'Is that a probe about my love-life?' she grinned.

'Of course.' His hands massaged her back with expert strength. 'I don't have to ask whether you were popular.'

'I've never had much time for men.' She shrugged as best she could lying down. 'I'm a working girl.'

'But you must have had dozens of boy-friends,' he prompted gently, rolling over on to his side and watching her with intense grey eyes.

'None of them ever affected me the way——' She choked on her sentence. The champagne must be going to her head! She had been about to say 'the way you do.' She cleared her throat. 'None of them really meant very much to me.'

'An ice-maiden,' he murmured. 'Yet you strike me as a very passionate woman, Alex.'

She flushed. 'Maybe the circumstances have to be right. I—I had an unfortunate experience once.'

'Go on,' he said with a lift of one eyebrow.

'Oh, it was nothing dramatic.' She paused, seeing Barry's face in her mind. 'I had a boy-friend once. He used to work at Carvel's. His name was Barry Dent. I—well, I thought he was something special.'

'And?' Anton was lying quite still, his eyes fixed on her with smoky attention.

'And he took me out for a drive one night, into the country. We stopped somewhere, to talk, the way young people do.' She grimaced suddenly, and picked up a handful of sand, letting it trickle through her fingers like an hour-glass. 'He wanted—he wanted more than I did.'

'He wanted to make love to you?'

'Yes,' she nodded slowly. 'I said no, and he insisted. I think he thought I was teasing, or playing hard to get. But I wasn't. I'd just realised, you see, that I didn't love him. He grew quite violent in the end. He even hit me once or twice.'

Anton said nothing, but gently stroked her cheek with his knuckles. Alex leaned her head against his hand briefly, pressing her cheek to him, and then sighed.

'I guess it was no big deal. That sort of thing must happen to a lot of girls. But we were miles from anywhere, and it was dark. I was terrified.'

'What happened?'

'A farmer happened to be coming across the fields with his dogs. He must have seen what was happening, because he yanked the door open and dragged Barry out. It wasn't very pleasant,' she said drily. 'The upshot was that Barry got the sack, and went up to

Manchester. The worst of the whole thing was that I'd trusted him.' She shook her head. 'I really did trust him.'

'And now?' Anton asked quietly.

'Oh, I don't think it's left me with any deep Freudian scars or anything,' she smiled. 'It just brought home to me that you have to look after yourself in this life. And that men can't always be trusted.'

There was a silence.

'I'm sorry, Alex,' Anton said at last. 'That shouldn't have happened to you.'

'It's long gone now. Funny,' she smiled, 'I've never told anyone that story. I thought it was buried too deep. A girl without a mother doesn't have anyone to confide in.'

'Until she marries,' he said gently.

'I guess so,' Alex said uncomfortably, and pillowed her face in her arms. 'So,' she said, her voice muffled, 'have you managed to psychoanalyse me?'

'I'm not trying to psychoanalyse you, Alex,' he said gently. 'Don't be so prickly. I just want to know you, that's all.'

'You know me better than anyone ever has,' she whispered into the sand. At first she thought he hadn't heard her above the murmur of the sea, but then she felt his lips brush the silky skin between her shoulderblades.

'That means a lot to me, Alex,' he said, and the husky timbre in his voice sent a thrill running along her veins. 'Now,' he went on, 'this is rest and recuperation time—and you're just about asleep. I'll wake you for some lunch in an hour.'

She lay blissfully in the warmth of the sun.

'You don't know how much better I feel,' she murmured lazily, 'getting that Barry episode off my chest.'

And then she was asleep.

It was a glorious day. When she woke, Anton had cold roast grouse and salads ready, and they ate with their fingers, sitting waist-deep in the creaming surf. Afterwards, they swam lazily in the calm water, then took the launch out for a circumnavigation of their little kingdom.

Alex had never been so happy, not since her childhood, at least. She found herself chattering gaily to Anton, delighting in his rather dry wit, revelling in the desire she always found in his deep eyes. Telling him about Barry Dent had somehow liberated her, putting an old ghost to rest. For the first time, she felt able to give her fascination with Anton full rein. She couldn't take her eyes off him. It was the first time she had really studied a man's body, apart from the clinical interest she had had as an artist and art-restorer, and she had never realised before quite how stunning a human physique could be.

Anton was in hard condition, not an ounce of spare flesh softening the lines of his body. At every movement, every turn, new muscles came into play under his velvety skin. As they wandered through the palm grove, hand in hand, she was fiercely proud of him, proud of being with him. Nothing mattered to her that afternoon, not Marina Bergatrice, not Anton's feelings towards her, not anything.

They were wading in a pool, looking for starfish under the rustling shade of a palm-tree whose roots were almost in the sea, when Alex suddenly yelped in dismay and sat down hastily in the warm, shallow water, clutching her heel.

'Trodden on something?' Anton asked, wading over to her.

'Yes,' she said through gritted teeth. 'Ouch, it hurts!' The pain was intensifying alarmingly, a burning needle-like jab in her heel.

Smiling, Anton scooped her up in his arms and carried her onto the sand.

'Now, let's have a look.' She bit her lip to keep back the tears as he studied her heel. 'Oh-oh!'

'What?' All she could see in the pink flesh were three little black dots. Surely they couldn't be the cause of so much pain?

Anton waded back into the pool and fished something out of the water, a little black ball of spikes like a tiny hedgehog.

'You've trodden on a sea-urchin,' he told her, showing her the little creature.

'Ouch!' she grimaced. 'It's not serious, is it?'

'No,' he said, squatting to look at her heel. 'But they usually hurt like hell. And if you don't get them out fairly quickly, they tend to fester.'

'Oh no! What are we going to do?'

'Well,' he said, 'we could go back to Venice and get some drawing ointment from a chemist.'

'But I don't want to go back yet!' she groaned, squeezing her ankle unhappily.

'Or you could let me do what the local fishermen do.' There was a gleam of amusement in his beautiful eyes.

'What do they do?' she asked warily. 'Ow, it burns!'

'You'll have to be a brave girl,' he warned her solemnly. 'It hurts, but I can promise you almost instantaneous relief afterwards. And it's a lot quicker and healthier than going to a chemist.'

'Go on, then,' she said, leaning back against the bole of the palm-tree. 'But I warn you, my pain threshhold is low!'

'Just relax,' he grinned. 'I'll be as quick as I can.'

Kneeling in the sand, he took her foot in strong hands, and lifted her heel to his mouth.

Alex watched in alarmed fascination as his lips closed over her pale-pink flesh—and then gasped in sudden pain as his teeth sank into the firm flesh on either side of the spines. There were tears in her eyes as he sucked hard, then spat out the little needle-point.

'Two more,' he said gently. 'Can you stand it?'

She nodded, not trusting herself to speak. Anton held her little foot firmly, and applied his lips to the second dot of pain in the tender skin. She gasped again, squeezing her violet eyes shut against the sudden, cruel pain. He didn't say anything this time, but after a second, extracted the last of the little thorns. Her heel was throbbing almost unbearably, and she melted forward against his broad chest as his arms slid around her. She fought back the sob in her throat, her long lashes wet with tears, as he rocked her gently, silently, in his arms.

The pain drifted out of her heel like water trickling out of a sponge. She opened her blurred eyes, and blinked down at her heel.

'Hey,' she said shakily, 'the pain's gone.'

'I told you so.'

There were merely three tiny dots of blood against the coral-pink now, and Anton wiped them away with his thumb. She was lying against him, cradled against his inner thighs, his arms close around her waist. With a little sigh, she laid her head back against his shoulder, closing her eyes again. Her long red-brown hair was spread out over his chest, its silky tresses warmed by the sun. Her beautiful, parted lips were trembling slightly; and she knew that he was going to kiss her.

His lips tasted delicately of sea-salt, but his tongue was sweet and warm, drawing a line of fire along the exquisite line of her lips.

Entranced, she felt his lips brush her eyelids, her cheeks, the soft skin of her temples, with butterfly lightness. They were silent. Only the rustle of the wind in the palm-leaves above, and the distant murmur of the sea broke the stillness.

When his lips met hers again, her arms crept up around his neck of their own accord, and she arched her throat to press her lips clumsily, tenderly, to his.

'I've never been at any other woman's feet before,' he said gently, brushing her silky hair out of her eyes.

'Anton,' she whispered, and with deep shyness, stretched up to give him an inexpert kiss, full on his passionate mouth. 'I'm not very good at any of this,' she said softly. 'I've told you—I never had much time for men. You must have had so many women, beautiful women, women who knew—all the right things to do. Why do you bother with me?'

'Don't be such a shrinking violet,' he smiled. His grey eyes, fringed with thick, dark lashes, were ineffably tender. 'You know very well that you're the most beautiful woman on this island.'

'Brute,' she whispered.

And this time his mouth was fiercer, more demanding. His skin was hot velvet against her, intoxicatingly sweet. She shuddered as he unfastened the catch of her bikini-top, his hands cupping her breasts as he buried his face in the cool skin of her throat. His lips found the beating pulses there, inflaming them.

'Anton!' she gasped again.

'Dear God, I want you, Alex,' he muttered, his voice husky with passion. She slid back on to the soft sand, and he followed her, his weight pinning her down as he covered her face with kisses.

His lips seemed to burn her ultra-sensitive skin, his tongue tasting the fragrance at her temples, in the soft hollow of her jaw, at the corners of her parted lips.

She clung to him, like a drowning woman clinging to a rock, her mind whirling into ecstasy.

'Sweet darling,' he whispered, 'I've been aching to do this ever since I first saw you at Castelnero, wandering like a lost child in a strange house . . .'

She could find no words to answer him. There could be no resistance now, no holding back. Her love for him was an overwhelming, surging power in her, a river that had burst its banks and was now gathering in flood. She wanted to tell him how she felt about him, tell him that she loved him beyond anything in the universe, but there were no words. She couldn't even begin to express what she felt.

Slowly, with agonising gentleness, he kissed the satiny skin of her collarbone, the first creamy swell of her breasts. Her fingers had knotted themselves in his dark hair, and she clung to him as his lips caressed the fragrant, delicate skin of her bosom.

She cried out softly as his mouth found the tender peaks of her breasts, his teeth and tongue firming them into tense points of desire. The feelings inside her were almost unbearable, and she was close to tears as he came up to hold her close, crushing her breasts against his chest.

'Darling . . .'

The shoulders she clung to were rigid with tensed muscles, and she could feel his desire against her, a bone-melting potency that made her gasp.

They lay in silence, embracing tightly, Anton's arms pressing her to him. Then with a deep, shuddering sigh, he relaxed, letting her breathe easily again.

'What is it?' she asked shakily. She could feel his tension, like the hum of power in a banked-down furnace. He kissed her softly on the mouth, his eyes full of passion.

'I don't want to be another Barry Dent,' he said quietly.

'You couldn't possibly be——' she denied.

'Oh, I think I could,' he said with a wry smile. 'You don't know how much I want you, Alex.' He drew a deep breath, running his fingers through his hair. 'I don't think I'm fully responsible when I'm around you.'

'Can't you see I want you, too?' she cried, his desire setting her aflame all over again.

'Yes,' he said gently, staring into her wide, hyacinth eyes, 'I can see that.'

'Is it because I'm so clumsy?' she asked miserably.

'Idiot,' he smiled, tangling his fingers in her hair and tugging, 'if you only knew how your clumsiness makes me want you!'

'It's Marina, then,' she said in a low voice.

'Don't be silly!' he snapped.

But something in his voice set alarm bells ringing in her head.

'It *is* Marina,' she cried.

For a second he was about to deny it. Then he shrugged.

'Marina comes into it. But not in any way you could imagine.'

'Try me,' she invited urgently.

'I can't.'

'Why not?' she demanded.

'Life is more complicated than you know,' he said wearily. A stab of pain shot through her heart.

'Do you—do you love her?'

'You're so innocent,' he said with a sad smile.

'But do you?' she demanded.

'That isn't a question I can answer, Alex.' His mouth had become a hard line.

And suddenly all the honey-sweet desire in her became a sick ache. The golden world around her crumbled into mist, and despite the heat of the afternoon, Alex shuddered uncontrollably.

'You do love her,' she whispered, almost to herself. 'And you're going to marry her.'

He watched her face with wise grey eyes.

'I don't suppose it would mean anything to you if I asked you to trust me?' he asked.

'No,' she said bitterly, 'it wouldn't. Barry Dent cured me of that folly years ago, remember?'

Anton winced. 'You don't know everything, Alex.'

'Oh, but I do,' she said savagely. The pain inside her was maddening her, making her want to lash out at him, punish him. 'I know everything about you,

Anton. Why you brought me here today. It was a cold, deliberate little exercise, wasn't it? Is this where you always seduce the servants?'

'But I didn't seduce you,' he pointed out calmly.

'Only because you want to see the butterfly wriggle on the pin a little more,' she said viciously, and again he winced. 'Maybe that's how you get your kicks,' she went on, unable to stop the cruel words from spilling off her tongue. 'Maybe you're not man enough to seduce them—so you just humiliate them instead!'

'I didn't mean to humiliate you, Alexandra,' he said angrily, his brows coming down warningly. 'You'd best stop now.'

'The truth hurts, doesn't it?' she snarled. 'I wouldn't be surprised if you didn't put that sea-urchin there on purpose—so you could enjoy inflicting a little physical pain for a change——'

She broke off with a sharp intake of breath as he reached out, his fingers knotting painfully in her hair. His eyes glittered with anger.

'If I didn't know you were overwrought right now, I'd put you over my knee and paddle your backside,' he grated. She stared into his eyes, shocked at his anger. 'Maybe that's what you've missed all your life,' he spat, letting her go, 'a father to knock the vanity and stupidity out of you!'

'That's a monstrous thing to say,' she said tearfully, struggling to put her bikini-top back on with trembling fingers.

'You've just said some pretty monstrous things yourself,' he reminded her grimly. 'Don't ever speak to me like that again, Alex.'

'I won't,' she said furiously. 'I'll never address another syllable to you again as long as I live!'

'Oh, lord,' he sighed, 'I didn't think you were the melodramatic type, Alex.'

'Didn't you?' she retorted, wiping the tears off her

cheeks with the backs of her wrists. 'Well, maybe you don't know anything about me.' She rose on unsteady legs. 'I said once you were like that winged lion, and that's what you are. You go crashing through other people's lives, taking what you want, always getting your own damned way, never caring who or how much you hurt!'

'Thank you for your expert analysis,' he said drily, rising, and brushing the sand off his legs. 'Have you finished?'

'And you don't ever look to see what the people around you are feeling,' she went on, ignoring him. 'You don't know how I felt about you, Anton. You'll never know, because you're incapable of any true emotion!'

' "Felt?" ' he queried quietly.

'You don't think I give a damn about you now, do you?' she asked with trembling scorn. 'I've discovered the truth at last, Anton—and I'm not ever going to be fooled again!'

'In which case,' he said grimly, 'I'd better take you back.'

'Please.'

She took a few steps, then stopped, rubbing the throb in her heel. He came up beside her, putting a supporting arm around her waist.

'Let me go!' she snapped, trying to shrug him off.

'Your foot will be too sore to walk on for a few hours yet,' he said calmly. 'You'd better let me help you.'

'I'd sooner stay here and rot,' she retorted, pulling away.

'God,' he sighed, 'your dialogue comes straight out of *Girl's Own Paper*!' He let her go, and walked off towards the launch.

The setting sun cast long, purple shadows across the sand of Paradise. Venice was a mauve and gold fairyland on the horizon.

Alex limped after him, her eyes wet with angry tears, trying to keep pace.

And every time her sore heel touched the sand, she whispered 'Damn—damn—damn!'

CHAPTER EIGHT

ALEX had wrestled with her pain and confusion all night long, and on Friday morning she awoke no nearer to a solution.

The one thing that was clear in her mind was that despite anything she had said to the contrary—and in the cool light of day she realised just how stupid her attempt to hurt Anton had been—she cared about him. Very much.

Love certainly hadn't come to Alex the way she might have expected it to—in a recognisable, pre-packaged form, easy to deal with, and full of sunshine.

Love was this churning turmoil inside, an ache, an ecstasy. A heady wine that was as bitter as it could be sweet. An impulse that drove her uncontrollably to be with Anton, and then drove her away from him.

As she soaped herself in the marble tub under the trailing pelargonium, she could only hope that Anton would measure the cruelty of her words to him against the depth of her feelings. Any other man, she knew, would have been turned off for life by her crazy outburst.

But maybe Anton de Cassis, with that intuitive brilliance, would understand her feelings.

Maybe.

She pulled on jeans and a pair of supple, much-loved boots. The slightly butch attire might help to give her confidence on this rather gloomy morning-after. But she left the checked lumberjack shirt open at the neck, showing just a hint of her breasts, and as an afterthought put on rather more *Joy* than her frugal habits usually allowed.

She considered herself in the mirror. Misery

certainly hadn't affected her appearance, she decided wryly. There were no grey hairs or bags under the eyes. On the contrary, the sun had gilded her fine skin, and her wide eyes, so deep a blue as to be almost ultramarine this morning, were sparkling-clear.

Yesterday's hours in sea and sun had bleached her hair very slightly, as they always did; and this morning there was more gold than red in the rich autumn tints. She applied a pale pink lipstick and a smudge of hazy blue over each eyelid. The result mightn't be the latest cover of *Vogue*, but it was undeniably attractive.

Slightly cheered, she went down to breakfast.

Anton's place was empty. A crumpled napkin and a cup still half full of black coffee showed that he had breakfasted early and briefly. A pang of remorse went through her. Had he also slept badly, and awoken depressed?

Bettina brought her grapefruit, cereal and coffee, and she ate alone in the magnificent dining-room, pretending to read a copy of *Il Mattino*, the morning paper. Half-way through breakfast, Umberto Borghese brought her a letter from Wilbert Carvel, containing a short congratulatory note and a cheque 'to buy yourself a present with'. That the normally Scrooge-like Wilbert should be giving out gifts six months from Christmas was an indication of his delight at her achievement.

'Umberto,' she said, folding away the letter, 'is Signor de Cassis out?'

'Not yet, *signorina*,' the old man smiled. 'I believe he is going to Switzerland later this afternoon. But for now he is in the study.'

'Switzerland?' she repeated in dismay. 'Thanks, Umberto.'

'*Prego, signorina.*'

As the secretary walked out, Alex dabbed her mouth with her napkin and rose hastily. If Anton was going to Switzerland today, then she wanted to speak to him before he left. To try and apologise. And to ask him to understand.

She walked quickly through the drawing-room to the study, trying to muster the words in her head. The slight twinge in her heel was a sharp reminder of just how bitter she'd been yesterday.

What *was* the relationship between Anton and Marina Bergatrice? Could he really be in love with her—or did she exert some other kind of fascination over him? Alex could well imagine that Marina Bergatrice would be sexually irresistible to many men; there was an almost decadent eroticism about her beauty and elegance that would fascinate men. Was that it? Or did she have some kind of hold over him, some influence that wasn't emotional, that couldn't be detached?

Suddenly she realised that she'd been very, very stupid. She hadn't the slightest idea *what* things were like between Anton and Marina. And she had been presuming to judge.

The study door was slightly ajar, and she could hear Anton's voice from within, talking on the telephone. She pushed through the door softly.

'Anton?'

He didn't hear her soft call. He was standing with his back to her, the receiver to his ear, staring out of the window at the sunlit canal outside. One hand was thrust into his jacket pocket, and the way he was standing somehow suggested tension, or anger.

'That's impossible,' he was saying, his deep voice rough with impatience. 'We had a contract, Herr Kohl. You can't change the terms now.'

He listened in silence for a while. Alex waited quietly by the door, watching him.

'You're talking about orders worth half a million,' he said angrily, half turning to consult some papers on his desk. Alex could see that his jaw was set and grim. the grey eyes dark.

'I don't give a damn about all that,' he said sharply, obviously cutting through the other man's sentence. 'Listen to me, Herr Kohl. If you default on this contract, I'm going to sue you for the total amount. Understood?'

He set the receiver down with a brisk click. Alex was about to speak, when he suddenly spun round, his eyes meeting hers with a glitter of sharp steel.

'What the hell are you doing here?' he snarled.

Shocked, she could only gasp, 'Anton——'

'What are you spying on me for?' he demanded, reaching her in two strides, and taking her elbow in a vice-like grip.

'I wasn't spying,' she said. 'You're hurting my arm, Anton! I just came to talk to you——'

'Will you do me a favour?' he snapped fiercely, his eyes full of thunder. 'Just keep out of my way, Alex. Do you understand that?'

'Yes,' she whispered, wide-eyed with horror.

'Then you can start right now,' he retorted. He let go her elbow, and without another word, turned back to the telephone.

Dazed, Alex walked out of the door, pulling it closed behind her, and walked up the stairs to her studio. Well, that was the end of her little dream. A deep depression settled on her shoulders, weighing her down. Her vicious tongue had destroyed the one thing she cared about most in the world. She had rejected the only thing she had ever truly wanted, and now she was paying the price.

An avalanche of misery unravelled steadily inside her. What a mess, what a stupid, pointless *mess*! She slumped into her chair in front of the Canaletto, and surveyed the half-cleaned surface with sightless eyes. There were no tears left inside her. Nothing but an aching void.

She picked up the scalpel she had been using, and slowly began to scrape at the thick encrustations of green paint on the hideous trees. There was a light footstep behind her, and she turned in her chair quickly. It was Anton, his face set and grim.

'Alex,' he said stiffly. 'I'm sorry.'

'Oh, Anton!' She jumped up to hug him, joyful.

A hard hand in her chest stopped her dead. His eyes were forbidding, his mouth strained into a tight line.

'Don't,' he commanded, and she fell back, dismayed. He drew a deep breath. 'I didn't mean to explode at you like that. I'm just very busy right now.'

'I understand,' she told him, her heart thudding. 'Can I—well, I know this sounds stupid, but can I do anything to help?'

'Just get that painting cleaned,' he said with a brief, tense smile. 'Anastasio d'Annunzio is coming to take a look at it later this morning. He's the Director of the Venice Art Foundation. Do you mind?'

'Of course not,' she said, still on edge at his brusque, cold manner.

'Good. I'll see you then.' He turned to go. 'I have a lot of things to do.'

'Anton——'

'Yes?'

'Umberto said you were going to Switzerland later today——?'

'Yes,' he said shortly. 'I have to see a man in Zürich.'

'When will you be back?' she asked timidly.

'Probably in the early hours of the morning,' he grimaced.

'Is anything wrong?' she ventured.

'A minor crisis,' he nodded.

'Look,' she said, clasping her hands nervously, 'about yesterday afternoon——' She gulped. 'I didn't mean all those crazy things I said.'

'Didn't you?' His smile was wry.

'Of course not. I was just so upset about——'

'Alex,' he interrupted gently, 'I don't have the time

for any complicated explanations right now. I'm due
at the Bank in ten minutes.'

'Oh!' she said, thoroughly snubbed.

''Bye.'

He was gone. Scarlet-faced, she sat back down at
her desk. What on earth was she going to do? Anton
very clearly wasn't in the mood for reconciliation.

Or maybe he just wasn't in the mood for Alex
Lacey. And maybe he wouldn't be ever.

As always, work gave her solace. Alex lost herself in
the technicalities of her craft, slowly cleaning away the
surface of the paint with meticulous care.

The emerging Canaletto was a masterpiece, pure
and simple. Of that she was completely certain. Even
at this stage, she knew that there wasn't another to
compare with it anywhere in the world. In scope, in
detail, in every respect, this was one of the most
majestic and beautiful paintings that Alex had ever
worked with. Only an expert eye could make sense of
the confused surface at this stage of the cleaning
process; but an expert eye would know unerringly that
this was one of the triumphs of Canaletto's art.

No date had yet emerged, but she guessed that the
work had been done in the late 1760s, just before
Antonio Canaletto's death, when the master's powers
were at their height.

Maybe—and her instincts thrilled at the thought—
this was the last work he had ever painted.

She was lost in the process of uncovering one of the
spires of the cathedral, when the door of her studio
opened, and Anton came in.

With him was a short, pale man with small, pale
eyes. And last of all, her sable coat open to reveal a
silver-and-black dress of stunning design, was the
Princess Marina Bergatrice.

The dark almond eyes met hers with cold hatred,
then narrowed in a false smile.

'Alex,' Anton said, 'I want you to meet Anastasio d'Annunzio. Professore d'Annunzio is head of the Venice Foundation.'

'How do you do?' Alex murmured, rising to take the pale hand.

Professore d'Annunzio's blue eyes lit up with a connoisseur's delight as they came to rest on the huge canvas.

'I am delighted to meet you, Miss Lacey,' he said in a tidy, precise voice, surprisingly deep in such a small man. 'May I congratulate you on your perception? This looks like being the fine art event of the year in Italy.'

'Discovering it was pure chance,' Alex smiled. Her eyes caught Marina's sardonic smile, and she knew that all three of them were thinking back to the ghastly afternoon of the discovery.

But Professore d'Annunzio was oblivious to any tension in the air.

'Magnificent,' he was muttering to himself as he leaned over the jumbled canvas. 'Truly magnificent. A great, unknown Canaletto!' He slid gold-rimmed spectacles onto the bridge of his nose, and pored over the painting, murmuring to himself.

Alex glanced up at Anton. The handsome face was still showing signs of tension, though his emotions were well banked down behind his normal, urbane manner.

'So,' said Marina, looking around the studio disdainfully, 'this is your little den, Miss Lacey?'

'How have you been, Princess?' Alex asked, unperturbed.

'In excellent health, thank you.' The glittering gaze swept her face, and Marina's eyes narrowed. 'You've been in the sun, I see?' she asked with a cold smile.

'I spent a day on the beach,' Alex answered mildly. She didn't want another scene at this point, and she didn't mention that the beach had been on an isolated island, and her companion Anton de Cassis.

'What do you think, Professore?' Anton asked. 'Is our Alex on the right track?'

'It's simply outstanding,' the Professor said, his eyes bright. He took a neat white handkerchief from a pocket, and mopped his brow. 'This is a wonderful work—I would guess from the master's later period. A wonderful work!'

Marina's face set into a harsh mask of suspicion.

'You mean it's a genuine Canaletto?' she asked sharply.

'Of course,' the Professor nodded, touching the surface with rapturous fingers.

'Why shouldn't it be a Canaletto?' Anton asked calmly, his eyes watching Marina's face.

'Bah! How can one tell, in its present mess?' She lit a cigarette, something Alex was beginning to recognise as a sign of tension. 'It looks like nothing on earth.'

'There is no doubt at all, Princess,' the Professor smiled. 'Anyone with an inkling of artistic knowledge would recognise the work immediately.'

For an instant, it looked as though Marina was going to contradict the art expert to his face. Then she changed her mind.

'So,' she said with an icy smile to Anton, 'your little friend is right. May I congratulate you on your good fortune?' The fury in the woman could be sensed, like an ultrasonic hum too high for human ears. Once again, Professore d'Annunzio was deaf to such inner tensions.

'The good fortune is not Signor de Cassis's alone,' he was saying happily. 'A discovery like this means good fortune for art lovers everywhere, for the whole world!' In a gesture which Alex guessed was highly uncharacteristic of such a neat, pale man, he took Alex's hand in both of his, and shook it vigorously. 'You have been very clever, *signorina*,' he told her huskily. 'Very clever indeed. My colleagues aren't going to believe it when I tell them just what a fine work this is!'

Marina had been watching with a tight smile, puffing at her cigarette.

'A clever little girl indeed,' she said sardonically. 'You must be very proud of her, Anton.'

'Oh, I am,' Anton said quietly. His eyes met Alex's for an instant, warm and intense, and she suppressed a shiver.

Marina's fury puzzled her. Surely the woman's jealousy couldn't extend that far?

Like other professionals in all fields, Alex always managed to keep emotional issues completely clear of her work. You simply couldn't afford to mix them. It was always a surprise to find how passionate lay people could become about artistic subjects.

And she was finding it difficult to believe that Marina Bergatrice could be so bitter about a great art discovery, simply because the person who had made the discovery was a rival!

'I'm so happy for you, darling,' Marina purred, patting Anton's cheek with a red-nailed hand. 'But now that you know it's a Canaletto, surely you're going to get a proper person to do the restoration?'

'Alex Lacey is a perfectly proper person,' Anton smiled gently.

'Oh, don't be silly,' said Marina with a tinkling laugh. She walked over to the canvas, and stared down at it through long lashes. 'I mean, honestly—*look* what this child is doing to it.' She gave Alex a gleaming smile. 'I don't mean any offence, of course,' she told her, 'but you have made a dreadful mess of it, haven't you, Miss Lacey?'

The blood rose hotly to Alex's cheeks.

'It happens to be in the middle of a very delicate restoration process,' she said stiffly.

'Oh, quite. Too delicate, surely, for you?' The

smile, as ever, was charming. 'You wouldn't want the responsibility of destroying such an important work, would you?'

'I'm simply obeying my client's instructions,' Alex replied, trying to keep calm. She would love to have slapped that insolent, patronising face!

'In my opinion,' Professore d'Annunzio said magisterially, taking off his gold-rimmed spectacles, 'Signorina Lacey is doing a superb job.'

'Really?' The good Professor didn't catch the smile of pure hatred that Marina threw him.

'Your concern is quite understandable, Princess,' he nodded. 'It is a great responsibility for one so young. But Signorina Lacey is eminently qualified. I have heard her very highly recommended by my English colleagues at the National Gallery.'

'And you think she's doing a good job?' Anton asked softly.

'An excellent job,' the Professor said firmly. He replaced his spectacles to study the canvas again. 'This is one of the most challenging assignments I've ever seen. And I don't believe I've ever encountered this precise way of solving it before.'

'Oh?' Marina's eyebrows rose.

'Would you mind showing us exactly how you're tackling this painting?' the Professor asked Alex.

'Not at all,' said Alex, still on her mettle despite the Professor's praise. The three people stood at her side as she picked up the cotton swab between a pair of steel forceps.

'The trick is to dissolve the later paint before the earlier paint softens too much,' she explained. 'I'm using a special cleaner—like this.' She swabbed a heavily-painted branch carefully, guiding the liquid over the textured paint. 'After a few seconds, I start wiping it out.' With a clean swab this time, she rubbed carefully at the canvas. The thick oil-paint smeared wetly, becoming a dirty brown blur.

'Now,' said Alex, watching it carefully, 'some pure mineral turpentine to take that away.' She mopped at the muddy patch, as carefully as a surgeon, then blotted up the residue with cotton-wool. Magically, as the brown disappeared, the gilt prow of a gondola was revealed where the branch had been. 'Voilà! That section has to be left to dry for a few minutes, and then it can be cleaned in the normal way.'

'Brilliant,' Anton murmured.

'Risky,' snapped Marina.

'That solvent you're using,' the Professor said excitedly. 'I've never seen anything like it. What is it?'

'It my own invention,' she admitted with a smile. 'It's a mixture of alcohol, various spirits, and some chemical thinners used in industry. It smells a bit peculiar,' she said, sniffing the familiar, sharp tang, 'but it's very effective.'

'You're very skilled with it,' the Professor conceded. 'Is it dangerous?'

'You mean to the canvas? Yes, it can be very dangerous. You have to work fast, because if it's left on for even a few minutes too long, it could penetrate right through to the underneath layers. And that would ruin the whole work for ever.'

'You shouldn't be using it, then,' Marina snapped. Her eyes were sharp and bright. 'You might destroy the painting in your inexperience!'

'I might,' Alex nodded calmly. 'But I'm afraid there are very few other ways of doing a job like this successfully. Some people try and scrape the surface layers off with a scalpel—I use that method myself now and then. But it invariably destroys a lot of the underneath paint as well. I've evolved this method especially for this kind of situation, where a more valuable work has been painted over by another artist.'

'You're remarkably calm about it all,' Marina sneered. 'Doesn't the value of the painting affect you at all?'

'Art restorers have to live with that, Princess.' She wiped her fingers clean on a rag. 'My philosophy, quite simply, is this—that the painting's been ruined in any case. If I can restore it, well and good. If not—then I leave it alone. I only do what I think I can accomplish.'

'I hate to interrupt such a fascinating conversation,' Anton said with a smile, 'but I'm afraid I have a plane to catch.'

'Of course, of course,' the Professor agreed, once again putting his glasses away. 'You're a busy man. Signorina Lacey, it's been a great pleasure meeting you. Keep up the good work—and I look forward intensely to seeing the Canaletto in its full glory. Goodbye!'

Marina Bergatrice stared broodingly at the canvas for a few intense seconds, then turned and walked out without sparing Alex a glance. Anton paused at the door.

'My plane leaves in an hour,' he told her. 'You'll be all right on your own?'

'Of course,' she smiled into his deep grey eyes. A sudden premonition of some kind made her shiver, as though something had disturbed the clear waters of her mind. 'Just come back safely,' she said urgently.

He raised an ironic eyebrow, then was gone.

Kitty Kowalski polished off the last of her *fritto misto*, a delicious mixture of batter-fried seafoods.

'That was del*i*cious,' she said firmly, 'though I'm glad I couldn't tell which bits were the octopus!'

'Nor could I,' Alex confessed. She glanced at her watch. Kitty's quick blue eyes caught the movement.

'You don't have to get back right away, do you?' she complained. 'It's only just eight o'clock.'

'I'm sorry,' Alex sighed. 'I just don't like leaving the Canaletto for too long when Anton's not there. And I wanted to do a bit more work on it tonight.'

'Sure.' Kitty poured herself a last mouthful of the dry red wine they had been drinking at the little *trattoria*, and then waved to the diminutive waiter for the bill. 'This one's on me,' she said firmly, waving away Alex's offer of money. 'Call it a celebration dinner. C'mon, I'll ride back with you in the *vaporetto*.'

The twilight was golden-rose on the water, and Alex lay back contentedly in the water-bus, drinking in the peace of the evening.

'That was a lovely meal, Kitty.' She reached and squeezed the American girl's hand. 'And I feel a lot better having got all that talk off my chest. 'I'm sorry, I always seem to be burdening you with my problems.'

'*De nada*. I enjoy these glimpses into the lives of the rich and famous.' Kitty smiled at Alex, and lit a cigarette, blowing a plume of luminous smoke into the sunset. 'Alex—about what you've been talking about tonight. Love and all that stuff.'

'Yes?'

'You know—love is just love, Alex. It's something that only happens to a woman once. Maybe twice if she's very, very lucky. But love isn't necessarily happiness. And it's not necessarily marriage with a swimming-pool and a four-door sedan. It's just itself. Are you following this complicated philosophy?'

'Not really,' Alex smiled gently.

'What I'm getting at is—sometimes a woman has to choose between love and lot of other things she wants. If the guy you happen to love isn't on the marriage market, for example. And if there happens to be another guy round the corner, who you don't happen to love. But who wants to marry you, with a swimming-pool and——'

'—and a four-door sedan.'

'Yeah. Well, in that case, you're going to have to choose whether you want love. Or whether you want marriage. Hell,' said Kitty impatiently, 'I'm not very good at philosophising, Alex. All I'm saying is that you can't always have things the way you want them. But believe me, love is a rare and precious thing. I guess you think me a pretty hard-bitten young case?'

'That thought had crossed my mind,' Alex said solemnly.

'Yeah. Nevertheless, I'm telling you, love is a rare and precious thing. Every woman has just so much inside her, waiting for the one Mr Right to pull out the stopper and set it free. And when Mr Right comes along, there isn't always time to stop and be sensible, and ask yourself whether your Aunt Agatha would approve. If it was me in your shoes, I'd take love every time.'

'And to hell with everything else?'

'And to hell with everything else. This is your stop, Miss Lacey.'

'Goodnight, Kitty—and thanks!' Alex scrambled out on to the 'pavement', and leaned back into the boat to call, 'See you tomorrow. And I might just take your advice!'

She walked up the grandiose stairs to the great door of Castelnero. At eight-thirty of a midsummer's evening, it was deliciously warm and balmy. She paused at the top step, enjoying the perfection of the moment. It had been good to get out of the house for a few hours and talk to irreverent, loveable Kitty. She watched the dying sunlight dancing on the water of the canal. Love, and to hell with everything? Maybe you're right, Kitty, she smiled, and let herself in.

Umberto Borghese was in the hallway as she closed the door behind her. He smiled a welcome.

'Did you have a nice meal, Signorina Alexandra?'

'Very nice, thanks, Umberto.' She pulled off her light cotton jacket, and slung it over one arm. 'Venice is beautiful at this time of day.'

'Venice has its moods, *signorina*, like a woman,' the

old man smiled. 'Shall I bring some coffee up to your suite?'

'Please. But I'll be in the studio, thanks. I want to do some more work on the Canaletto.'

'Ah, *signorina*,' said Umberto, 'you are doing such wonders up there. Your presence in this house transforms everything into sunshine.'

'Why, thank you,' Alex said gently. 'That's a lovely thing to say.'

'Some women bring darkness into a man's life,' Umberto told her in a quiet voice. 'Others bring sunshine.'

Alex smiled, thinking this was just another bit of Venetian gallantry. Then she stopped.

'You mean—Marina Bergatrice?' she said slowly.

'Yes, *signorina*. That woman brings an atmosphere of darkness with her.' He sighed heavily. 'If she never set foot in this house again, it wouldn't be too soon. I'll bring the coffee up in a minute.'

She turned to go, nodding, then stopped again, an uncertain feeling creeping over her.

'Umberto——'

'Yes, *signorina*?'

'Was she here tonight? Marina Bergatrice?'

'Yes, *signorina*,' the old man said in surprise. 'She came just after you went out. She had left her gloves in your studio this morning.'

'In my——? Oh, God!'

Alex dropped her coat, leaving the old secretary gaping after her, and ran up the stairs, two at a time.

CHAPTER NINE

THE door of the studio was locked. She had left the key in it when she went out.

Fool!

There was a spare set of keys in Anton's suite, she knew. Alex raced down, her heart pounding in her chest, and burst into the deep red rooms. On her way back up, the ring of keys clattering her hand, she met a grey-faced Umberto, who had been labouring up the stairs after her.

'For God's sake, *signorina*—what is it?'

'I don't know,' she cried, fumbling with the keys. 'Something's wrong with the Canaletto!'

'Wrong?' The old man groaned as she fumbled the key into the lock. Twisting it with panicky haste, she threw the door open and ran in.

'Oh, no!' She bit her knuckles to stop the scream.

The huge canvas was lying on the floor, as though it had slid off the table.

Except that it couldn't have slipped. Unless someone had pushed it.

And lying on the middle of the painting was an empty bottle of the solvent. The deadly solvent, that could eat right through oil paint in minutes. Now spread in a huge puddle right across the surface of the Canaletto and over the floor.

'Oh, *signorina*,' Umberto Borghese groaned, wringing his hands, '*che disgrazia!*'

Alex stood rigid, trying to control her horror. Think, think! When had she gone out? She looked at her watch. An hour and a half ago. If Marina had staged this 'accident' just after she had left, that meant the solvent had been lying on the delicate surface for over an hour at least.

160

And it destroyed oil paint within minutes. Dear God, she had said exactly that in front of Marina Bergatrice, in this very room, a few hours ago. She herself had planted the seeds of this terrible act in Marina's dark mind!

'*Signorina*——' Umberto's eyes were wet with an old man's tears. 'Is it ruined?'

'I don't know,' she said, her voice sounding oddly calm. The pool of solvent was brown and sticky with the paint that it had dissolved. She did know. No oil paint could have survived that prolonged attack.

Under that sticky pool would be nothing. Nothing but the grey of the canvas that had once held one of the world's treasures.

'Let's call the police,' Umberto was saying urgently. 'That woman must be arrested——'

'Who would believe that she did it?' Alex asked, her voice still crazily calm. 'No one in the world would think that this wasn't an accident. An accident caused by my negligence.'

'No!'

'I'm going to see what I can do,' she said quietly. 'The solvent hasn't covered the whole canvas. Perhaps the edges of the painting can still be salvaged.'

'*O, Dio,*' the old man said weakly, leaning against the wall. 'A masterpiece! Worth countless millions of lire——'

'Not any more,' said Alex in that mad, calm voice. 'Umberto, will you bring me that coffee, please.'

'Coffee?' the old man mumbled. He brightened slightly at the prospect of having something to do, and shuffled out. Suddenly he was ten years older, his white face blank with shock.

Alex stooped and lifted the bottle of solvent off the sodden canvas. The plastic stopper, supposed to be spillproof, was lying in the far corner.

They would say she had simply failed to put it back properly.

Marina Bergatrice would say it for them.

She knelt, and picked up the great canvas by its wooden stretchers. The evil brown mess quivered as she lifted it, a rivulet sliding off one corner to splash against her shirt. She didn't notice.

The catastrophe had paralysed something in her mind, depriving her of emotions. Later, she would find tears for a great masterpiece destroyed by a warped mind. Tears for her own reputation, stained for ever.

Tears for Anton de Cassis.

But for now, she felt nothing, her heart and brain numb. She laid the painting down on the desk and switched on the spotlights. The ruby glow of the sunset was filling the room with blood.

With unfeeling fingers, she pulled a fistful of cotton-wool off her pad and sponged at the edges of the great brown stain.

Ironically, there were still traces of Antonio Canaletto's drawing on the canvas. Like the bones of a corpse that the scavengers had done with. She wiped again.

That wasn't a drawing. That was the paintwork— Canaletto's paintwork. Shaking her head against the impossible, she wiped elsewhere. A blue sea, bright with gondolas and barges, appeared from beneath the brown puddle.

'Dear God,' she heard herself whispering, 'let it be a miracle——'

Carefully, she wiped again, blotting up the sticky mixture of pigment and solvent, and discarding the sodden pad.

Her throat was suddenly dry, her breath rasping painfully. *The painting was still there.* But it couldn't be. She rubbed her eyes hard. It was no illusion.

She tried to keep the hope from springing up, but it surged in nonetheless. She snatched up a handful of cotton-wool and blotted gingerly at the brown stain. Dear heaven, there it was! The Canaletto was still intact, incredibly, unbelievably intact. Only the Victorian over-painting was damaged.

But how on earth could that have happened? That solvent should have turned the oil-paint into mush over an hour ago—Unless . . .

Alex sat back weakly. Unless the Canaletto——

Suddenly her emotional paralysis broke, and she gasped out a laugh that was three-quarters a sob. Of course! The Canaletto wasn't an oil painting at all! Like so many of his contemporaries, Canaletto had painted this masterpiece in egg tempera. Beautiful, glossy egg tempera, brighter than oil paint, though thinner. Much more difficult to handle, but stunningly beautiful in the hands of an expert. A mixture of powdered pigment with the most ancient medium of all, water, a little oil, and an egg-yolk. Vulnerable to water.

But not to turpentine, alcohol, or thinners.

With trembling hands, Alex wiped away the heavy brown stain. She wasn't sure whether to laugh or cry, but her relief was so great that she felt she could have leaped out of the window and flown among the primrose-and purple sunset clouds.

Marina Bergatrice was in for a great disappointment. And a very unpleasant surprise. Alex shook her head, still slightly numb. How could she have done something like this, simply to spite a rival in love? It was unthinkable, the savage act of a poisonously distorted child. She could see right through Marina's plan now. After the destruction of the Canaletto, she would make sure that Alex's reputation was gone for ever, her career ruined, and any possibility of an affair between her and Anton de Cassis utterly crushed. She would point out to Anton that she had warned against letting Alex restore the work in the first place. She would have won, hands down.

'Not this time,' Alex whispered, rubbing a little linseed oil on to the canvas to take off the last smears of solvent. In fact, with a bitter irony that Alex could now enjoy, Marina's 'accident' had actually done nothing more than finish the job Alex had so meticulously started. Almost every trace of the Victorian over-painting was now gone, and as Alex cleaned away the mess, the full, breath-taking beauty of the Canaletto underneath was emerging.

The door creaked open and Umberto Borghese shuffled in, his head bowed over the tray of coffee he was carrying.

'Here, *signorina*,' he said dully, looking up at her with broken eyes. Then they lit on the Canaletto, glowing in magnificent colour under the spot-lights.

The tray slid out of his fingers, and a Sèvres coffee-cup splintered on the floor.

'It cannot be?' he exclaimed in disbelief.

'It is,' Alex said gently, coming to take his arm. She led him to the wonderful painting. 'There. Isn't it superb?'

Together, they stared at the exquisite thing in awe. The great cathedral dominated the panorama, as Alex had guessed it would. The square in front of it, painted with a sweeping perspective, was crowded with people. Behind, the beautiful buildings along the Procuratie Vecchie rose up against a summer sky. The sunshine in the painting, the atmosphere of Venice in midsummer, was breathtaking.

'*Madonna*,' the old man whispered. 'You have wrought a miracle, *signorina*!'

'Not me, Umberto. The Princess' plan misfired—it ended up doing good, not harm. There are still the outer edges of the painting to be cleaned, though.' She turned to the old secretary, who was tearful with relief. 'Umberto, you packed a bottle of champagne for our picnic lunch the other day.'

'Yes, *signorina*—there are several cases more.'

'Just one bottle will do,' she smiled. 'Will you take a glass with me?'

Umberto was already trotting out of the door.

'With the greatest of pleasure, *signorina*,' he chuckled, and went to fetch it.

There was really little more to be done. Marina's efforts had removed the surface layers more brutally than Alex would ever have dared, but no less effectively for that. Within an hour, the great canvas was ready to be put back into its ornate Baroque frame—heavy, beautifully-carved giltwood, and itself a minor treasure.

The champagne had made her slightly lightheaded by the time she was sealing the Canaletto back into the frame with strips of copper. She felt weak, giggly, and a little weepy.

What was Anton going to say when she told him the ghastly story? If he believed her, surely that would mean the end of anything between him and Marina? At the thought of Marina, a shiver passed through Alex.

That woman was sinister, even evil. She would never be able to regard the Venetian princess with equanimity again. A woman's jealousy she could understand—but this attempt to kill a beautiful, wonderful thing was sickening.

Back in its frame, the Canaletto was overwhelming. Alex propped it against the wall, and sat back in her chair with the last of her champagne to study it.

What was Anton going to do with it? The appearance of a painting of this importance on the art world's horizons was going to cause a minor earthquake. If it were ever put up for auction, it would fetch an immense sum. Maybe one and a half or two million pounds. Certainly nothing less. Galleries and private collectors all over the world would be competing for it. And no one would ever know the close escape this masterpiece had had. No one except herself and Anton. And Marina Bergatrice.

The sleek cream telephone on her desk burred, and she picked it up.

'*Signorina?*' Umberto's voice was agitated. 'A call from the Princess Marina! Shall I say you are out?'

'No,' she said immediately. 'Put her through, Umberto.'

'Hullo? Miss Lacey?'

Alex's heart was beating hard, but she kept her voice calm.

'Hullo, Princess,' she answered. 'May I help you?'

'Thank you. I want to leave a message for Prince de Cassis. Will you tell him to ring me first thing tomorrow?'

'Of course,' Alex said calmly. 'Nothing else?'

'That's all,' the cool voice said. 'Is everything—all right at Castelnero?'

'Yes, thank you,' said Alex with a quiet grin. 'Why—should anything be wrong?'

'Not at all,' the Princess said sharply. She hesitated. 'How is the restoration work going?'

'Very well indeed,' Alex replied in a mild voice. There was a silence. Then the light voice came down the line again.

'No problems?'

'No, none. I'm sitting in front of the Canaletto right now, as a matter of fact,' she said. 'It's finished, you know.'

'Finished?' Marina's voice was sharp. 'What do you mean, "finished"?'

Alex grinned again. In a tone of slight surprise, she

said, 'Why, completed, of course. The restoration work. It looks very beautiful.'

In the silence that followed, Alex could imagine the thoughts whirling round inside Marina's head. A wicked sense of amusement made her add, 'There was a very slight accident.'

'Yes?' The monosyllable was strained.

'Somebody was clumsy. But it all worked out for the best in the end.'

'I see.' The note in Marina's voice told Alex that she knew she had failed. 'Congratulations, Miss Lacey. I expect to see you very soon.' The receiver clicked.

The cold fury in Marina's parting remark wiped the smile off Alex's face. That Marina knew she had failed, no matter how, made her all the more dangerous. She sat thinking hard for a few seconds, wishing she hadn't spoken to the Venetian woman after all. Then she shrugged.

'Well,' she murmured to the great painting, 'I'm certainly not leaving you alone again tonight. You're coming to my bedroom!'

She lifted the heavy painting and carried it out of the studio, down to her bedroom. She laid the beautiful thing against the wall opposite her bed, so that she could look at it, then sat down on the bed, her knees weak.

The past few hours had been somewhat nerve-racking.

And she was just in the mood for an early night. She crawled gratefully between the sheets. The ivory tints of the bedroom were infinitely soothing. She lay propped against the pillows, staring at the painting with unseeing violet eyes, trying to make sense of the day's events.

Oh, Anton, she thought with a wave of loneliness, why aren't you here? She had never missed him so much, had never been surer of her love for him. If only he were with her now, those strong, sure arms around her, that passionate male mouth pressed to her temple, the way they had lain in the sand at Bresolo.

Switching off the bedside lamp, Alex rolled under the sheets. A shivery ache in her bones warned her that a slight fever was on its way. Exhaustion smoothed out the lines of her face, and she was dimly aware of tense muscles twitching as they relaxed into sleep. In her mind's eye, his face was before her, his smile wonderful . . .

She awoke sweating, feeling as though she were strangling. Coughing painfully, she tried to sit upright. *Smoke*.

Her senses screamed at her. She clawed at the light-switch in panic. When the light clicked on, it revealed that her bedroom was filled with acrid, suffocating smoke. She stumbled out of bed in horror. Castelnero was on fire. Dimly, she could hear a muffled roar from beyond her bedroom door.

Fighting back the violent coughs that racked her, Alex stumbled to the door and pulled it open. The Ivory Suite was also billowing with white smoke. Through the suffocating clouds she could see a dull red glow at the bottom of the outside door. The door was burning. She was trapped in the suite. Slamming the door wildly, she ran to her bedroom window. The smoke was burning her eyes terribly as she struggled with the catch, and tears streamed down her face. At last she got it open, and flung the sash up, leaning out into the fresh night air.

The courtyard was down below. Gasping in the oxygen, she peered with smarting eyes for a way down. There was none. For the first time, real fear gripped her. She drew in her breath to scream, but only a retching cough came out. Gasping for air, she slid on to the floor.

And for the first time she became aware that the air in the suite was hot. The very wooden floor on which she was sprawling was hot.

Where were Umberto and Bettina? She clawed her way upright, and leaned out of the window again.

'Help!' she called. 'Help! Fire!' Her voice was barely a hoarse croak. The silent Venetian night mocked her. Dear God in heaven, couldn't anyone *see* that the house was on fire?

She stumbled back to her bed and snatched up the bedside telephone. By her alarm clock, it was two-thirty in the morning. Hysterically, she rattled the buttons on the instrument. There was no answer. Not even the dialling tone. The fire must have melted the cable. She flung the instrument aside and fumbled through the acrid smoke for her dressing-gown, tying it clumsily around her flimsy nightie.

At all costs she must get out of this suite, or she would suffocate here, long before the flames reached her. The house was still eerily silent, but for the distant rumble of the flames.

The Canaletto! Pulling a blanket off the bed, Alex bundled the great canvas into it. Another fit of coughing seized her as more smoke entered her lungs. Her chest was horribly raw and painful, as though it were burning too. She tried to think of everything she had ever been told to do in a fire. Nothing came to mind.

Clutching the painting, she hesitated in fear. It was too high to jump from the window. She would be smashed on the stones of the courtyard, forty feet below.

She would have to go through the door to her suite. Her heart failed her.

'Come on, Alex,' she whispered to herself, 'come on, girl . . .' She gathered her long hair into an untidy bun. Wet towels! In the bathroom, she ran water clumsily over all the towels she could find. She wrapped one around her hair and her mouth and nose, like a burnouse, and draped the others, around her shoulders. Then, picking up the Canaletto, she ducked her head, and stumbled through into the smoke-filled drawing-room.

She could feel the heat from behind the door as she got near it, coughing painfully. The bottom panel, heavy old oak, was glowing red. With a spasm of horror, she realised that the door might be the only thing holding the flames back. She hesitated for a moment, clutching the painting. The swirling fumes made her gag horribly, deciding her. Some fragment of common sense made her wrap her hand in a corner of a wet towel before reaching for the brass doorknob. The metal hissed against the moisture as she tugged. For a second, the door resisted, then it came open with a shower of sparks.

Alex screamed as a huge buffet of super-heated air swept her against the jamb. She clung there, gazing with terrified eyes at a scene from hell.

The whole corridor was ablaze, a river of fire. It was terribly hot, hot enough to shrivel her tender eyes and scorch her face, a hungry heat that licked at her like the breath of some immense, monstrous predator. The roar of the flames was deafening, a constant explosion that sucked the oxygen from the living air, and spewed out poisonous smoke in return, like a giant bellows.

Beyond the corridor, Alex could see the landing in a shimmer of heat. By the red glare of the flames, the stairs seemed intact. But the floorboards were fluttering long yellow streamers of fire, and as she stared out, a single tongue of flame licked up the curtains at the far window. The frame exploded into a square of fire, and with a splintering of glass, the entire window began to give way.

Like the lungs of some monster inhaling, the fire sucked a fierce draught of air in through the broken window, then let it out in a hungry roar that redoubled the heat of the flames. Fire streaked up the walls, tearing out the silk wallpaper and shrivelling it into ashes within seconds. The furnace-heat made Alex stagger back, gripping at the painting with terrified hands.

She was on the second floor of the house. There were still two levels below her. Did she have even the ghost of a chance of making it alive?

Without thinking, she plunged out into the corridor, and ran for the landing. The heat was unbelievably intense; it was like the inside of a furnace, the cone of a volcano. Flame snatched at her with cruel hands as she stumbled through the pile of ash that was all that was left of the carpet, and collapsed on to the stairs, the painting tumbling from her hands.

The very marble was hot, and the dry, scorching air was almost completely devoid of oxygen. Opening and shutting her mouth desperately in the shimmering air, Alex sucked with useless lungs at the super-heated atmosphere.

Dizzy with heat and lack of air, she fumbled the Canaletto into her arms, and clambered down the stairs.

All her movements now seemed to be nightmarishly slow, like some insane kind of dance. A dance of death. Her lungs heaving in the rushing, blistering air, she rounded the turn of the stairs. A glare of white heat rose to meet her.

The first floor was ablaze, too. The whole centre wing of Castelnero was one great funeral pyre. She sank to her heels on the hot marble. The fire-wind licked the tears off her cheeks as soon as they spilled out of her burning eyes.

Below her was a sea of fire. Almost nothing of the rooms was visible, just a waving field of flame. There was no way through. She clung to the painting, staring into the heart of the flame.

Thank God you're not here, she said to Anton in her mind. That sea of flames was your room. Thank God you're safe, at least.

A groan like that of some huge creature in pain rose above the roar of the flames. She looked up. The second-floor landing was giving way. The fire had destroyed its strength in an incredibly short space of time. As she cringed back against the stairs, a huge beam sagged out of the flaming woodwork, and fell with a fountain of sparks into the floor below. For an instant the flames were blotted out in a billowing cloud of black smoke as the great oak beam smothered the fire. Then, steadily, the fire burst into life around the wood, and reached up again. Alex choked into her towel as the poisonous smoke swirled around her. But the glimmering of an idea had dawned in her mind. She peered up with red-rimmed eyes. Another beam, some twenty feet long, had begun to sag out of the flames above. She poised herself for flight, watching its progress desperately. With a great rending crash, the beam plummeted down, landing among the flames below like a rocket. Instantly, Alex jumped down into the thick smoke. In the few seconds that the flames were extinguished, she might have a chance of reaching the stairs below.

In the whirling black cloud, her ankle caught on something.

A searing pain wrapped around her leg, and she stumbled among the coals of some piece of furniture. At once, the great pyre burst into life around her, its red and yellow arms reaching for her.

With a soundless scream, she sprang back, holding the painting to shield her face, and thudded into the wall behind her. She could smell her own scorched eyelashes and eyebrows, and she beat hysterically at the flames crawling up the towel she had pulled around her shoulders.

Ominously, it was now bone-dry.

The great bonfire had now hemmed her into a corner. To both sides of her, the corridors were raging, impassable. In front of her the landing was pouring flame and smoke up into the upper sections of the house, devouring the splendour of Castelnero. And, trapped in her little alcove, Alex was at its mercy. She was there for the fire to take, at its mad whim. She crouched against the panelling, fighting down her panic.

This was surely the end. She flinched in fear as another immense beam from above plunged down-wards, the impact of its landing gushing sparks and coal in all directions. Now she had only seconds to live. Seconds of searing agony. She squeezed her eyes shut, trying to pray.

'Alex!'

She opened her eyes in disbelief, squinting against the fierce heat of the flames. Anton was thrusting the blazing baulk of timber aside with an axe. Through the quivering heat-haze, she could make out the strain on his face.

Numbly, she tried to rise to her feet. The beam slithered aside with a crash, releasing a gout of flames. Oblivious to them, Anton leaped through the heart of the fire towards her. She stretched out her arms, calling his name with scorched lungs.

'Anton! Oh, thank God——'

Then he was with her, his arms tight around her.

'Darling,' he called above the roar of the fire, 'are you all right?'

'Just—a bit weak,' she gasped. His marvellous solidity was wonderful. She clung to him desperately, digging her fingers into the hardness of his muscles. The jacket he wore was scorched and smouldering,

and the face she loved so much was made a savage
mask by sweat and black ash.

'Can you walk?'

'I don't know,' she gasped. The pain in her ankle
had become fierce, and she was horribly weak. He
lifted her gently to her feet, shielding her from the
consuming heat with his body.

'Alex, we've got to get out of here.' His voice was
commanding, urgent. She tried to muster her
strength, nodding her understanding. He pointed to
the wall of flames before them. 'We're going to have to
get through that. Okay?' Roughly, he rearranged the
towels around her flimsily-clad body, and pulled her
close to his side, wrapping his own jacket over her
face. 'Now!' he shouted. 'Come on!'

She let him drag her forward, her feet stumbling.
The heat enveloped them in agony, sucking the air
from their lungs, tearing at their flesh. Her knees
buckled, and he jerked her savagely to her feet.
Then they were in a billowing darkness of acrid
smoke. The painting fell from her fingers as she
coughed agonisedly. She dropped to her knees to
grope for it.

'Come on, for God's sake!' Anton shouted, his fingers
knotting in her hair as he reached blindly for her.

'The painting,' she croaked, 'the painting!' Her
fingers found its smooth surface, buried in the warm
ash, and she grabbed at it wildly as Anton hauled her
forward.

The blackness exploded into another inferno of
white-heat, a shooting ordeal of flame, and she felt
something huge smash into Anton's shoulder, sending
them both sprawling.

His fingers were like a vice around her wrist, pulling
ever forward, through the pain and terror of the
flames. Her mind was numbed, unable to cope with it
all.

And then hands were reaching for them, lifting

them, guiding them into a misty heaven where the air was breatheable, and where the devouring heat had eased a little.

Alex was choking, trying to call Anton's name. Voices around her spoke urgently in Italian, and through bleary eyes, she caught a glimpse of two orange-uniformed figures in helmets dragging fire-hoses towards the flames.

She slumped on to a blanket on the marble floor of the hall. Someone held a mask over her nose and mouth, and she heaved to get the oxygen into her lungs. Then she thrust it away.

'Anton——' she croaked.

'I'm here, darling.' The arms that cradled her were infinitely strong, infinitely tender. She touched his blackened face with shaking fingers.

'You're alive,' she whispered.

'And so are you.' He gently kissed her dry lips. A single tear spilled across her cheeks, making a white track through the soot on her face. He eased the towel away from her head and neck, and her magnificent auburn hair tumbled out around her shoulders.

'Anton,' she breathed, 'I love you. I love you . . .'

The soft darkness was rising up to claim her. Willingly, she let herself drift. And welcomed the oblivion that eased away her suffering, her fear, her weariness

She was more than half asleep as they dressed her burns—which were miraculously few. Apart from the burn to her ankle, and a number of bruises and abrasions, she had come through the ordeal without injury.

They let her sleep until mid-morning—'for observation'—and then woke her so that the doctor could check her lungs. She sat patiently forward, her chemise rolled up, as the cold disc of the stethoscope roamed across her ribs. Then the doctor unhooked the instrument from around his neck with a satisfied nod.

'Very good,' he smiled, patting Alex's arm. 'No sign of any inflammation. That's the most common injury after fires, you know—smoke damage to the delicate tissues of the lungs. I would just take it easy for a few days.'

'Was—was anyone else hurt in the fire?' she asked nervously.

'No one. The staff were apparently out for the night.'

'And Anton—Signor de Cassis?'

'We treated him for minor burns last night.' He smiled. 'But we discharged him after treatment. As we are about to discharge you.' He leaned forward to study Alex's eyes. 'No sign of any headaches? Nausea? Confusion of any kind?'

'None,' she said. 'I'm being discharged, you say?'

'Yes,' he nodded. 'Signor de Cassis is coming to collect you in a few minutes. There's no reason to keep you here any longer. If you get any signs of delayed shock, just get straight into bed and keep warm. And no alcohol. Okay?'

'Okay. But——'

'Your eyes are really a remarkable colour, Signorina Lacey,' the doctor said thoughtfully. 'Did you know that they're almost violet? The colour of hyacinths, I would say. Very attractive. With that Titian hair, very striking indeed.' His professional manner reasserted itself. 'Well, I must get on to my other patients.'

'But I haven't——'

He bustled out, and Alex slumped back against the pillows. Discharged? She hadn't a thing to wear except her dressing-gown, which had been scorched irreparably. And there were a million things she wanted to know!

The nurse who had dressed her wounds last night came in with a telegram.

'For you, *signorina*—from England.'

She opened the envelope in puzzlement. It was from Wilbert Carvel:

CONGRATULATIONS YOUR LUCKY ESCAPE STOP BRAVE GIRL STOP YOUR LEAVE GRANTED AT ONCE STOP HAVE A WONDERFUL TIME MUCH LOVE FROM US ALL

She blinked at the words. Leave? She hadn't asked for leave. And where was Anton? She wanted to speak to the nurse. She was about to reach for the bell-push, when the door of her room opened. And her heart did its familiar slow somersault backwards.

'Anton!'

He bore not the slightest trace of having walked through an inferno in the small hours of the morning. The incredibly handsome face was impassive, and he was dressed in an immaculately-cut charcoal suit, with a fresh white carnation in his buttonhole. His deep grey eyes glinted as he laid the parcel he was carrying down on her bed.

'Feeling better?'

'Fine, thanks.' Her throat was dry. 'And you?'

'A few scratches.' His smile dazzled her, carving those sexy lines at the corners of his mouth. 'Well, are you ready to leave?'

'But, Anton,' she protested, 'I haven't anything to wear. All my clothes are at Castelnero——'

'I've brought you some things.' He indicated the parcel. 'I hope you like them. You'll have to do a lot more shopping in France, I'm afraid. Just about all your things were burned in the fire at Castelnero.'

'France? Burned?' Bewilderment made her blink. 'What do you mean?'

'I mean that we've had enough of Venice for the time being. Almost all the bedrooms at Castelnero were burned. Only the ground floor rooms are intact. Which is just as well, since all the precious things in the house were there—but I'm afraid you and I have nowhere to sleep, no clothes to wear, and no roof over our heads.'

'What are you planning to do?' she gaped.

'We're going to the South of France. Not to Antibes, I'm afraid,' he smiled, his eyes bright, 'but to somewhere a lot quieter. I've got a house at Ste Maxime, near St Tropez. You'll like it.'

'Anton, I—I don't know what to——'

'Rest and recuperation,' he said firmly. 'Ste Maxime is really just a big village. There's the sea, the Alpes Maritimes, lots of sunshine, beaches. It's ideal. Now please don't argue, Alex—just get dressed. Ste Maxime is barely an hour's flying time from here, but our flight leaves in an hour and a half.'

Leaving her astonished and gaping, he rose, a tall, magnificent figure whose eyes were alight with humour.

'Come on, Alex. I'll be waiting for you outside.'

She watched him stride out, then fumbled dumbly with the package before her. *Ste Maxime?* The wrapping unfolded, revealing an exquisitely lacy bra and matching pants. Underneath was a suit in cream silk, cut with the flair that only a top fashion designer could bring to such a classical garment. White stockings, a navy-blue blouse, white silk scarf. And a pair of hand-made dove-grey court shoes. Everything exactly her size. In her stunned state, she found time to reflect wryly that Anton de Cassis had bought clothes for women before.

She dressed as quickly as she could, excitement rising as the reality sank in. The South of France, with Anton!

'Look,' she burst out as she pushed through the door of her ward to meet him, 'there are a million and one things I want to ask——'

'You can ask them this afternoon—at Ste Maxime,' he said, taking her arm. 'Did everything fit?'

'Yes. How did you know my sizes?'

'I've got a good memory,' he said with dry smile. 'Let's get down to the taxi. We don't want to keep the plane waiting. Do we?'

CHAPTER TEN

THE wind sighed gently in the tall pine-trees that shaded the marble terrace. Alex leaned against the balustrade, and stared with rapt violet eyes at the beautiful vista below—a sun-baked and wild garden that unfolded down to a sweeping crescent of white beach and blue Mediterranean sea. A huge tumble of bougainvillea spilled in purple-flowered glory off the edge of the terrace.

'I knew you'd like it,' Anton said gently. 'We'll go for a swim later on, and then have a quiet dinner *a deux* in the villa.' He unhooked his tie and opened his silk shirt to expose that velvety-skinned chest.

'This is heaven,' she sighed, tearing her eyes away from him to glance up at the primrose-yellow villa behind them. 'A swim? But I haven't got a bathing costume any more!'

'The beach is very private,' he smiled, and she blushed uncomfortably.

'Anton,' she said, 'there are so many things I want to know——'

'Such as?'

'Where's the Canaletto now?'

'Anastasio d'Annunzio has it. It's quite safe with him.' He came up beside her, and slid a strong arm round her waist, pulling her close. With a tremor, Alex laid her head against his shoulder, and stared down through her lashes at the blue sea below. 'I'm selling it to the Venice Art Foundation.'

'I'm glad,' she murmured. 'A treasure like that should be available to everybody.'

'Quite,' he said solemnly. 'Also, I need the money.'

'You?' she queried. 'Impossible!'

'Not so impossible,' he contradicted gently. 'If that fire had destroyed the Canaletto, I would now be in a very serious situation.'

'You mean—that minor crisis you were talking about?'

'Yes. There are a lot of things you don't know, Alex. And I wasn't able to tell you. You were too busy working on your precious Canaletto—and falling in love—to notice all the wheeling and dealing that was going on around you.'

She looked up at him quickly, her heart missing a beat.

'How do you know I was falling in love?' she demanded.

'I want to tell you a little story,' he said, ignoring her question. 'About how Telescan came into being. At twenty-eight, I was a young man with a lot of bright ideas and no money, Alex. That's a common situation. I had some revolutionary new designs for telecommunications equipment, and I knew how to devise the technology to put my ideas into practice. What I didn't have was a backer. Someone to finance my theories, and put up the money—a lot of money—to make it all come true.'

She listened, fascinated, watching his beautiful face.

'I came to Venice, to see my uncle at Castelnero. He was enthusiastic—in his rather eccentric way—but he didn't have any spare capital. Only Castelnero. But he put me in touch with a very wealthy Venetian businessman. A man called Prince Carlo Bergatrice.'

'Marina's father?'

'Exactly.' He caressed her long, silky hair absently. 'Carlo was prepared to put up the money. But he wanted a very big cut of the profits—leaving me only half. I agreed, and within six months, Telescan was under way. In three years, Carlo and I were millionaires. My uncle died, and I inherited Castelnero. It was in a pretty dilapidated state, and in

a rather foolish mood of quixotic optimism, I decided
to restore the house to its former grandeur.'

'All destroyed now,' she murmured compassionately.

'I'm very well insured,' he smiled. 'The structure of
the house is undamaged, and reconstruction work
starts next week. But restoring Castelnero was my first
mistake. It cost a tremendous amount of money,
leaving me very vulnerable financially. Then Carlo
Bergatrice died. His only child Marina inherited his
estate in full—including half-shares in Telescan. But
that wasn't enough for Marina. She wanted more.'

'She wanted you?' Alex asked quietly.

'She wanted the whole of Telescan. Getting me
would have been merely a step towards that goal. And
Marina is a very clever, ruthless woman.'

'I know,' Alex shuddered. Anton pulled her close.

'To cut a long story short, Marina offered me a
choice. Either to marry her, and unite all the shares in
Telescan. Or else she would take it from me by force.'

'By force?'

'Economic force. I was badly over-extended after
the restorations at Castelnero. I had barely anything of
my personal fortune left. Marina took advantage of
that situation to try and put me out of business. She
used her contacts and influence around Europe to
force some clients to cancel important orders.'

'Like Herr Kohl?'

'Like Herr Kohl,' he agreed with a quick smile.
'Normally, the situation wouldn't have been serious. I
could have sorted out the cash-flow crisis from my
own account until all the contracts were honoured.
But at that particular time, there wasn't anything in
my account. I had no money to cushion myself against
the blow. Marina had a vast personal fortune at her
disposal. She was planning to run Telescan into the
ground for a few months—long enough to buy up all
my shares, and then refloat the company under her

own flag. Leaving me penniless. I was short of a million and a half pounds to protect myself.'

'And then the Canaletto turned up,' said Alex, the situation slowly becoming clear in her mind.

'You turned up first,' Anton corrected her gently. 'A beautiful, adorable girl from London, who arrived like a ray of sunshine in all my darkness.'

Alex gulped.

'A girl who went straight to my heart as no other woman had ever done. I couldn't get you out of my mind, Alex. You fascinated me, possessed me . . .'

'Anton,' she gasped, clinging to him as he crushed her in his arms.

'No,' he said huskily, 'let me finish my story first, darling.' He drew a deep breath. 'When Marina saw what was happening between you and me, she became insanely jealous. She demanded that I marry her at once, or she would destroy Telescan utterly. It was then that you found that Canaletto. And Marina and I knew at once that her threat was nullified. The value of the painting was easily enough to tide me over the crisis—and to foil her plans completely.'

'So she tried to destroy it,' Alex whispered. 'I didn't tell you, Anton—there hasn't been time. But Marina came to Castelnero, and tried to destroy the Canaletto——'

'I know,' he nodded. 'Umberto telephoned me in Zürich—I was trying to raise money from a finance bank there. As soon as I heard, I came rushing back to Venice. To try and stop the second attempt.'

'The second——?' She stared up into Anton's dark eyes, dawning horror making her cold all over. 'Oh, God! You mean that fire——'

'Was Marina's little idea. Yes.'

'I can't believe it,' she shuddered. 'She could have killed me, could have killed dozens of people!'

'Marina comes of Venetian doges who once ruled half of the East, Alex,' he said wryly. 'Remember that winged lion you said I was like? Well, that's the spirit that made Venice great. The spirit which moved Marina Bergatrice to act as she did.'

'Dear heaven, how terrible!' Her cheeks were pale with shock. 'Can you prove it?'

'My business is telecommunications,' he smiled gently. 'Castelnero is fitted with a hidden closed-circuit TV system to protect it against burglars. My own invention. It's highly secret equipment, all miniaturised, and only Umberto Borghese and I knew it was there. The films clearly show Marina starting the fire on the first floor of Castelnero.'

'What will happen?'

'The film is with the police. So is the Princess Marina.' He ran his fingers through her autumn-red hair, smiling down at her. 'At the moment, I don't really care what happens to Marina. I guess with a top lawyer she'll get a short sentence. Maybe even a suspended sentence. But the films will be enough to persuade the Telescan stockholders that Marina Bergatrice isn't a fit person to run the company. She'll be forced to resign, and sell her stock. She no longer has any power over me or my company.'

'I thought you were in love with her,' Alex whispered still shaken by what he had told her.

'The only woman I've ever loved—and ever will love—is you, Alex.'

His kiss was a shuddering delight that possessed her, took her completely. She clung to him, her love for him pulsing through her body like fire in her blood.

'I love you, Anton,' she said with a sob, pressing her face against his broad chest. 'I've loved you since that night in the Hall of Mirrors, when you kissed me under the chandeliers.'

'I love you, my darling,' he said huskily, his mouth caressing hers, roaming over her face with intoxicating kisses. 'I love you . . . love you . . .'

The Mediterranean sun poured its golden heat down on them, and a light breeze rustled the bougainvillea flowers on its way from the aquamarine sea to the baking land.

'Anton,' she said softly, pulling back to study him with hazy violet eyes, 'don't be too harsh on Marina. I know you think she was only after your company. But I think that in her own way she really did love you. I can't imagine any woman not loving you. Maybe it was her love for you that drove her to do all those terrible things.'

'What makes you so sympathetic to Marina all of a sudden?' he asked with a loving smile.

'She's a woman. Like me. And I know what it is to love someone who seems not to care about you. It's enough to drive anyone mad . . .'

'I love your gentleness,' he whispered, kissing her face with thrilling passion, 'I love your compassion, your beauty, your sexiness——'

'Oh, Anton, I want to belong to you, I want to be so utterly yours that nothing and no one could ever take the smallest atom of me away from you!'

'That's how you're going to be,' he promised, the certainty in his deep eyes matched by the strength in his arms. 'Which reminds me—I promised to bring you something from Zürich. I want you to put it on now.'

The diamond blazed in the summer sunlight as he slid the ring on her finger. Dazzled by the fire in the stone, by the sun, by the beauty of the world around her, she stared up into the face of the man she loved more than anything in the universe.

'I'm technically a resident of Ste Maxime,' he smiled tenderly. 'And Monsieur l'Abbé du Barry is an old friend of mine. He's going to be only too delighted to perform the service. I'm arranging it for Saturday. Too soon?'

'Anton——'

His lips closed on hers, one hand reaching up to caress her cheek, sliding down her slender neck, to rest with heart-jolting possessiveness on her breast.

'But Saturday's tomorrow!' Alex gasped weakly.

'We can spend this afternoon choosing a wedding dress,' he said calmly, his eyes melting her very soul with their intensity.

'No ... Not this afternoon,' she whispered. 'The doctor in Venice told me that if I showed any signs of shock, I was to go to bed at once. And keep warm.'

He threw back his head and laughed. Then he kissed her hard, full on the lips, and scooped her up in his arms, and carried her up through the scented garden to the villa.

'I'm going to keep you warm,' he promised. 'All the days of your life.'

Take these 4 best-selling novels FREE

ANNE MATHER
born out of love

VIOLET WINSPEAR
time of the temptress

CHARLOTTE LAMB
man's world

SALLY WENTWORTH
say hello to yesterday